Bello:
hidden talent rediscovered

Bello is a digital only imprint of Pan Macmillan,
established to breathe new life into previously published,
classic books.

At Bello we believe in the timeless power of the imagination,
of good story, narrative and entertainment and we want to use
digital technology to ensure that many more readers
can enjoy these books into the future.

We publish in ebook and Print on Demand formats
to bring these wonderful books to new audiences.

About Bello:
www.panmacmillan.com/bello

Sign up to our newsletter to hear about
new releases events and competitions:

John Buxton Hilton

John Buxton Hilton was born in 1921 in Buxton, Derbyshire. After his war service in the army he became an Inspector of schools, before retiring in 1970 to take up full-time writing.

He wrote two books on language teaching as well as being a prolific crime writer – his works include the Superintendent Simon Kenworthy series and the Inspector Thomas Brunt series, as well as the Inspector Mosley series under the pseudonym John Greenwood.

John Buxton Hilton

GAMEKEEPER'S GALLOWS

First published in 1976 by Macmillan

This edition published 2012 by Bello
an imprint of Pan Macmillan, a division of Macmillan Publishers Limited
Pan Macmillan, 20 New Wharf Road, London N1 9RR
Basingstoke and Oxford
Associated companies throughout the world

www.panmacmillan.com/imprints/bello
www.curtisbrown.co.uk

ISBN 978-1-4472-2941-4 EPUB
ISBN 978-1-4472-2940-7 POD

Copyright © John Buxton Hilton, 1976

The right of John Buxton Hilton to be identified as the author of this work has been asserted in accordance with the Copyright, Designs and Patents Act 1988.

Every effort has been made to contact the copyright holders of the material reproduced in this book. If any have been inadvertently overlooked, the publisher will be pleased to make restitution at the earliest opportunity.

You may not copy, store, distribute, transmit, reproduce or otherwise make available this publication (or any part of it) in any form, or by any means (electronic, digital, optical, mechanical, photocopying, recording or otherwise), without the prior written permission of the publisher. Any person who does any unauthorized act in relation to this publication may be liable to criminal prosecution and civil claims for damages.

The Macmillan Group has no responsibility for the information provided by any author websites whose address you obtain from this book ('author websites'). The inclusion of author website addresses in this book does not constitute an endorsement by or association with us of such sites or the content, products, advertising or other materials presented on such sites.

This book remains true to the original in every way. Some aspects may appear out-of-date to modern-day readers. Bello makes no apology for this, as to retrospectively change any content would be anachronistic and undermine the authenticity of the original. Bello has no responsibility for the content of the material in this book. The opinions expressed are those of the author and do not constitute an endorsement by, or association with, us of the characterization and content.

A CIP catalogue record for this book is available from the British Library.

Visit www.panmacmillan.com to read more about all our books and to buy them. You will also find features, author interviews and news of any author events, and you can sign up for e-newsletters so that you're always first to hear about our new releases.

Chapter One

In 1875, at the age of twenty-seven, Thomas Bramwell Brunt had not yet blossomed into that full flower of eccentricity that was to be the hall-mark of his maturity.* But already the buds of individualism were beginning to burgeon. His suit was of poor quality cloth and he wore it aggressively badly. His face had begun to sprout an asymmetrical crop of warts, pimples and sebaceous excrescences. And he had just been promoted, at a remarkably early age for the time, to the rank of sergeant in the criminal investigation division of his county force. He had also, much to his disgust, been transferred away from the congeries of mining towns in eastern Derbyshire where he was held in almost legendary awe.

Why had his inscrutable masters behind their mahogany desks decided to waste his abilities on the wild moors and empty hills, under the even wilder and emptier skies of the High Peak Hundred? He saw nothing to convince him that the open spaces were likely to be fruitful for a plainclothes policeman with his way to make. On the other hand, Tom Brunt understood a knife between the ribs after a drunken brawl in Clay Cross or Ilkeston. A skull stove in under a rhapsodically swung crow-bar on a slag-heap behind a winding-engine, and Brunt was there, slowing down emotions and events to the pace at which he could record them in his laborious note-book. And although he was not a man of physical stature, he would eventually turn up at the Station arm in arm with some black-jowled giant, at whose aspect the men in uniform stood well back behind the massive solidity of the counter in the public office.

*See *Rescue from the Rose*, Macmillan 1976.

The story – or rather the stories, for there were two of them – for which he was sent haring out into the north-west desolation of the shire, struck him essentially as the sort of drivel that was turned up when Chief Constables and their more rarefied aides started dabbling in work that would have been more safely left to their underlings. Somebody needed to point out, gently but finally, that the case of young Amy Harrington was poppycock; but that was hardly a suitable role for a detective-sergeant, especially a new one, and the Superintendent – who ought to have shown better concern for a subordinate's time – had sat through the Chief's rigmarole as if he thought it was inspired. Even in the office afterwards, while Brunt was desperately trying to pass on the details of half a dozen unfinished cases to overworked colleagues, the Superintendent remained apparently convinced.

'Obviously the Turkish pedlar business won't lead you far, Brunt – but it does give you an excuse to go there. And just you find Amy Harrington.'

A fortnight ago, Brunt might have back-answered, but his new seniority rested uneasily on him. It needed to be protected until both he and other people were used to it. Becoming a sergeant had actually made Brunt nervous.

All the same, the case of the Turkish pedlar was, believe it or not, already more than a century and a half old. Whereas if anybody really wanted to bring back Amy Harrington, there were stews and lodging-houses in Derby and Nottingham where it would be more useful to be looking than amongst the wastes and dry-stone walls.

Even Brunt's physical journey into the remoteness of the Peak had invited catastrophe after catastrophe. Missing by a minute and a half the only useful train out of Derby Midland, he had arrived at the southern terminus of the Cromford and High Peak three-quarters of an hour after the departure of the only train of the day that accommodated passengers. But this in itself, he gathered at Cromford Wharf, need not necessarily discourage him. Even the time-table scheduled no less than five hours and twenty-five minutes for the thirty-three-mile journey to Whaley Bridge* – and this was if all the stages in the complicated journey could be made to interlock. Conceived in the first instance, improbably, as a canal (which was why some of its stations were still called wharves) the project had become a railroad in the very earliest days. It rose to well over a thousand feet above sea-level, and at five points along the route trains had to be hauled up hair-raising gradients by stationary engines. In each case further progress depended on the next locomotive being where it ought to be to haul the wagons along the next stretch. It seldom was.

'If it's the Fly you're wanting, you ought to be able to catch her up at Sheep's Pasture Incline. They generally hang about there a bit.'

But Brunt, carrying a suitcase that had benumbed both his hands, arrived at the foot of the slope in time to see the three trucks and the single passenger coach receding over the summit in a cloud of gritty smoke. He slogged on foot up to the Ashbourne Turnpike, in time to see the Fly's rear buffers vanish into the Parsley Hay cutting. The train was now away on a sixteen-mile stretch between inclines, and short of an actual breakdown of the locomotive, he had no chance at all of catching it. He got himself a lift on a carrier's cart, leaving himself another nine miles or so to complete on foot.

All for Amy Harrington. Yesterday morning Brunt had called on the Harringtons: at least, here he felt on familiar ground. Brunt, who could predict the movements of Tapton to the man and to the minute, knocked on the miner's door at the one moment of the day when he knew he would be immobilised, as nearly at a psychological disadvantage as he was ever likely to be: in his hip-bath on the hearth-rug five minutes after the last pair of clog-irons had echoed along the cobbled terrace.

Harrington looked over his shoulder as his wife said the single word *Police*, the whites of his eyes staring out of the coal-dust with the enquiring rage of a stalled stallion.

*Readers wishing for further details of the extraordinary working of this line are referred to A. Rimmer: *The Cromford and High Peak Railway*. Locomotion Papers No. 10. The Oakwood Press.

'The name is Brunt: Sergeant Brunt.'

'Tha'll have found her, then?'

'I'm still open to persuasion that she's lost,' Brunt said. 'In any unwilling sense.'

'She isn't there, is she? Tha's been to Piper's Fold?'

'Tomorrow,' Brunt said, intending neither to apologise for his delay nor to explain it. 'And how long's she been working there?'

'Since last back end.'

'And she's seventeen? So it wasn't her first job?'

'This was her third place. She went into service when she was twelve.'

There was an angry challenge in his tone, and Brunt knew all that it implied. Harrington's wife, a lean woman in the voluminous black rags of poverty, had long since abandoned any pretence to appear feminine. She went on scrubbing her husband's back as if they did not have a visitor.

'Amy was always a good girl,' Harrington said, countering an allegation that had not been made. Brunt could imagine the woman repeating, thirty times a day since the girl had disappeared, that it came as no surprise to her. She poured water down the miner's back from a broken-handled jug, made no effort to speak for her daughter's reputation.

'So where did she first go to work?'

'Old Eleanor Copley's, over on Mellor Brow.'

'For a year?' A girl often did take her first position near home. It was supposed to be a tempering of the wind before she went into one of the bigger houses further afield; in hard fact, as the only pair of working hands in an impoverished establishment, it was often the worst year of her life.

'Then she went to the Alloways at Rowsley. They own the ring-spinning mills at Ambergate. Between-maid. There three years.'

'How often did you hear from her?'

'Twice a month, regular. Till she went to work for this Captain Kingsey. She'd write one Sunday night, Mother the next.'

Doubtless there was some old crone in the street somewhere

who would decipher the girl's letters, and act as scribe to the mother.

'Then it dropped to once a month, once every six weeks, two months. Mothering Sunday she didn't come home. Other years she hadn't missed, choose what time she'd had to take the road. And always brought a simnel cake.'

'Piper's Fold to Tapton's no easy hop,' Brunt said.

'She could have done it if she'd wanted to.'

'So perhaps she didn't want.'

The woman turned for her husband's towel, refusing to be stung into any revelation.

'So when the letters stopped, you wrote to Captain Kingsey?'

It must have been an excogitated effort, drafted by the best brain at the pit head.

'He wrote back and said she left them on the 23rd of April, dawn early, and took all her things with her. As well as some of his. And that's what I know is not true. Show-piece valuables, he said. Irreplaceable things. Of course, if she ever did turn up again, there were charges that would have to be made.'

Yet Kingsey hadn't notified her missing, had laid no information.

Harrington stood up, his broad back to Brunt, luxuriating with the fierce heat of the fire on his genitals.

'I know what goes on at these places.'

'Generally speaking, you mean – or do you want to lay a particular complaint against the Captain?'

Harrington hawked out a throatful of coal-streaked sputum which hung on the fire-bar until it was dried out like a twist of animal membrane. He reached up to the mantelshelf for a wad of grimy letters.

'Read that, then.'

The one on top: immature handwriting, black thumbprints in the margin.

The Captain dressed me up like a girl in one of his old pictures and next week he is going to let me help him in his studio.

Harrington spat again: artists, studios. Useless to argue with his prejudices. He had been round to the Station and made a report to the Tapton Sergeant that had caught the fancy of the top brass. And the Chief had thought this an opportunity to show Harrington and his friends that the law could be on their side, too.

'You must understand, Mr Harrington, if a young woman of your Amy's age decides to up sticks . . .'

'Our Amy's a good girl, Mr Brunt. She never left a place without a character. Else Kingsey wouldn't have taken her, would he?'

Brunt was not so sure. A girl without a character, even if it were withheld out of malice or caprice, had little to choose between poverty, dishonesty or prostitution. Sometimes she did get another place, even though it was known that her character was not all that it might be – and then the implications might be even more unhealthy. Brunt looked at Mrs Harrington.

'And what are your thoughts about all this?'

'She wouldn't have taken anything that wasn't hers.'

Whatever else she did? Those were the words that she did not add; but she knew her own daughter, and it was savage knowledge. The Harringtons had a framed text over the mantel: *We are the people of his pasture and the sheep of his hand.*

The next morning. Brunt went over to see Eleanor Copley, over on Mellor Brow, a scraggy old harridan whose neck tendons stood out scrawnily under greying lace. He looked more than once at the current holder of Amy Harrington's first job: another thirteen-year-old from one of the mining villages: white faced, hair trailing out of its clips, nostrils raw, falling over her own skirts in elastic-sided boots.

'Amy? She was a good girl.'

She would hardly have said that if she had not intended to qualify it in the next breath.

'But fine ideas.'

'Such as?'

'She spent all her time dreaming. I suppose it was ideas she had. I used to say to her, *sit on a cushion and sew a fine seam*, but it might be as well to get your hand in with a row of blanket-stitch, first. They're all dreamers, girls nowadays. They dream of being whisked out of the corner in a fairy coach.'

'That can happen to some,' Brunt said. 'Especially if they're prepared to keep their eyes open for their own pumpkin.'

But Eleanor Copley would not bite on that bait. She was a woman without rapport with anyone. And the visit made Brunt miss his train, still without any satisfying image of the girl he was supposed to be looking for.

He rested his suitcase and looked at the roof-line of a row of cottages, the hamlet of Old Harpur, still some two or three miles away. There he would meet up again with the Cromford and High Peak Line, and though there were no more trains today, he would at least be able to walk along the track. It was, in fact, the only way in which he could reach Piper's Fold. There was a road of sorts by which one could come into the village from the Staffordshire side, but that would have entailed a detour of some twelve miles. From this approach, the community was accessible only to feet or hooves.

Piper's Fold: 502 inhabitants, according to the latest count: one church; one country residence; a farm or two; a dozen or so trial lead workings, scarring the hillside, all either exhausted or abandoned; a wooden platform Halt on the Cromford and High Peak, and that a mile and a half's walk from the first outskirt cottage. God knows why anyone decided to settle there – or how anyone had managed to subsist by remaining.

The railway line brought Brunt scant reward, its grass banks too uneven to walk in comfort, its sleepers too far apart to stride, the ballast between the rails loose and painful under his feet.

Piper's Fold: a farm or two; a bleak gentleman's residence that could only have appealed to a recluse beyond the perimeter of sanity. And yet the village had its piece of memorable if inglorious folk-lore.

In 1712 – a hundred and sixty-five years before the disappearance of Amy Harrington – a Turkish pedlar had come over the hills. Even the nationality of the man had been a matter of assertion rather than proof. Perhaps he had a certain Eastern Mediterranean exoticism in his looks; perhaps there was a certain Ottoman flavour about the silks and furbelows, the cameos and enamels, which spilled out when he lifted the lid of a pack almost too heavy for him to carry. There were also strange insignia – crescents and scimitars – on some of the coins in the leather bag which he wore on whip-cord round his neck.

One of these coins was at this moment lying snug in Brunt's waistcoat pocket, a five-piastre piece, one from a collection which had recently appeared in the showcase of a man called Isaac Mosley, a dealer in curiosities in the very centre of Derby itself. It was to serve as an outward and visible sign of Brunt's ostensible reason for coming up to Piper's Fold at all. It so happened that Isaac Mosley had had in his possession other property which it had been possible to identify more precisely. He was duly charged and convicted as a receiver of stolen goods, but stubbornly declined to give any account of those articles which were clearly of Balkan origin. But Brunt's Chief Constable was an imaginative man with a penchant for picturesque old legends.

This particular tale insisted that it had been on a glorious day in mid-February, with a spell of unexpected sunshine playing on dew-ponds and shed-roofs, that the Turk had come up the shallow valley now followed by the C. and H.P. There must have been a very convincing forecast of spring in the air, for the wives and elder daughters of Piper's Fold made some successful demands on the purses of their men-folk. The Turk's leather bag bulged. And another man in the Fold to do well out of the visit was the landlord of the inn, *The Crooked Rake*, at which the Son of the Prophet spent part of the night.

But only part of it; the next morning his body was found half an hour's walk out of the village, close to where the railway now ran, his throat gaping from the clean sweep of a knife, his leather bag hanging empty outside his shirt. His coffer, also relieved of its contents, was discovered partially hidden under loose stones, half-way between the inn and the corpse.

In the early eighteenth century, Nemesis appeared to have worked relatively slowly. But at last suspicion fell on one George Beresford, an ostler, who appeared later in the year arraigned before Queen Anne's Justices at a court convened in *The Crooked Rake* itself.

No watertight case was ever proven, but the story was handed down with certain strong assumptions: that the witnesses had proved impenetrably unhelpful; that there had been an understanding between the ostler and a kitchen-maid called Kitty Malkin; another between the landlord and the ostler; and yet another between the landlord and the toddy-sipping Bench. George Beresford was acquitted and the village was reluctant to discuss the matter further.

Until, that is, the first anniversary of the crime: another February day, but one truer to the Pennine seasons, with snow slashing across the fields in horizontal arrows, and more of it promised in huge banks of yellow cloud across Axe Edge. That evening, another Turk arrived: a swarthy figure with sleek hair and ebony moustaches. But he did not open his pack – in fact, the women kept to their cottages. Nor did he reveal the contents of any leather bag he might have about his person. And hardly had he sat down to his supper than his brother arrived – or, at least, a man demonstrably of the same blood – and within an hour or so, two pairs of cousins so that, by an hour before the normal bedtime of Piper's Fold, half a dozen Turkish pedlars were monopolising the inn fire, since most of the male drinkers had, it seemed, opted to go early back to their own hearths, pleading the imminence of a fresh blizzard.

Blizzard or no blizzard, the Turks did a vigorous night's work. Amongst other activities, they built a cairn on the spot where their compatriot had last looked on the waning moon. It was a lasting monument, to become a landmark on the line between Harpur Hill and Ladmanlow. Moreover, despite the inclemency of the night, three other people made the uninviting journey up to Pedlar's Stump: the landlord, the ostler and the kitchen-maid, all of whom were found with their backs against the cairn, their heads almost severed frontally from their throats. A cordon had been drawn round them: a circle of whip-cord stretched round stakes driven into the snow, from which hung an odd assembly of small creatures: rats, stoats, weasels and an unnaturally frozen crow; a signal such as lyrically minded gamekeepers display as a warning to other vermin.

All of which had been assiduously recorded by Sergeant Thomas Brunt in his note-book, as nearly as he could get them down in the words of the Chief Constable himself. Brunt's lumpy features had betrayed no reaction whatsoever during the telling of the tale.

Chapter Two

Brunt was taken off balance before he had gone many more yards along the track. Wishing to change his bag from his right hand to his left, he hopped across the rails so that it was now his left foot that took the sleeper ends and his right foot the grassy bank. And it was at that moment that he heard the clank of metal behind him, the squealing of brake-shoes on iron wheels and the sudden escape of built-up steam from protesting cylinder-cocks. A light engine had come up on him and screamed metallically to a halt with its front buffers less than six feet behind him. Every creaking, oil-dripping joint, every sweating tube and hissing pipe seemed to unite in indignation. And from the driver's cab there leaned a man in blue overalls whose ferocious eye-brows wandered, jutted forth, threatened, spread this way and that at alarming angles, asked furious questions and rejected in advance any answer that they might receive. Brunt carried his bag round to the flank of the engine and looked meekly up at this character, the eye-brows now splayed in incredulousness at the effrontery of a direct approach. He was a burly man, in his early fifties, with close-cropped hair and a streak of oil across his forehead.

'Can you give me a lift into Piper's Fold?'

'Not into Piper's Fold, I can't, because the line doesn't bloody go there. But I can put you down at the bloody Halt.'

He pushed open his little metal door and Brunt swung himself up the steps on to the foot-plate, struggling awkwardly with his suitcase. The driver stretched down a hand under his shoulder-blade and lifted him into the cab. Brunt found himself in an atmosphere of heavy oil, of acrid coal-dust and metal polish on gleaming brass handles, of intolerable heat attacking him through the cracks in the badly fitting fire-box doors. The driver pushed up the regulator handle and they jerked into motion with an ear-splitting roar from the smoke-stack. The fireman threw open the fire-doors and evened out the roaring coals with a flat rake: an even bigger man than the driver, though rotund rather than brawny, with an enormous head that seemed too massive for his shoulders.

There was not really enough room on the footplate for three men. Brunt found it hard to place himself so as not to be in the way of elbows, legs, flailing boots and shovel-handles. It was impossible to move because of the miscellany with which the cab was packed. Behind him, leaving only a narrow gap through which coal could be got from the tender, was a stack of wooden crates, one of which contained a pair of ferrets. Jammed tightly between two of the boxes were a twelve-bore sporting gun and the sections of a greenheart pike rod. Perhaps this was why the Fly sometimes reached the summit of one of its notorious Inclines to find its expected engine temporarily engaged elsewhere. Even entertainment of the passengers seemed possible, for on a hook on one of the crates, between a mole-trap and a brass telescope, hung a concertina.

The driver lessened steam, put gentle pressure on his brakes, and shouted something to his fireman, who seemed well aware what was expected of him. With one foot against an iron step he hoisted his huge bulk nimbly on to the tender, picked up a vast boulder of coal as easily – and almost as lovingly – as if it had been a baby, cradled it tentatively in his arms for a second or two, then launched it through the air, over the wall into the yard of a cottage they were passing. A man came out of a shed and waved an arm in acknowledgement. Then the steam was off again, the brakes grinding down. They came to a standstill miles from anywhere. Brunt looked out at a broken gate leading into a field – a weathered shoal of exposed stone – an acre from which no man could hope to wrest a living.

The driver began to turn down brass handles all over the bewildering console of the boiler, looked up at the pressure gauge; a wisp of steam was escaping from an inefficient joint lagged in old sacking. The driver reached for his shot-gun. The fireman opened the door at his own-side of the cab and jumped down.

'Look after her for us, then, mister. Know what to do if she blows off steam?'

'No.'

The driver looked at him incredulously.

'Know how the injector works?'

'No.'

The driver patiently stood his gun against the tender.

'If the safety valve blows, inject water into the boiler. Cool her down. Take the pressure off: see here—'

He dived for a tap, somewhere amongst the battery.

'Open your water. Open the injector here a shade. Wait till you've got a cone of steam and you hear it take the water up. Then crack her out wide.'

He fiddled confusingly with one tap after another.

'You'll be all right. Don't worry if she does blow. She may not explode this trip. If she does, we'll be in earshot.'

He dropped himself out of the cab. The two men went off on separate errands. Brunt was left alone on the footplate, the monster hissing, throbbing, humming, trickling – seething with pressure and life. He tried to remember the handles that the driver had indicated, touched one or two of them, then began to look with professional habit at some of the other articles in the cab: a wicker bait-basket, an enamel tea-can, a hessian holdall for bits and pieces, marked with the owner's name in home-spun print: *Thos Beresford, C. and H.P.*

George Beresford, ostler, Piper's Fold, a hundred and fifty years ago: arraigned, acquitted and his throat cut; Thos Beresford, 1875, machine-minder of the new age: it made sense. And how long between them? How many generations? Five, six? Thos Beresford, born when? 1820? His father, say, 1790? So George Beresford, ostler, murderer and murdered, might have been this man's great-great-grandfather? Might even also have been remarkable for his eye-brows?

Behind the fire-box door, the coals were raging furiously. Brunt identified the water-gauge, a tube behind brass-lined glass panels. He was not sure how it worked, but the level looked pretty low to his layman's eyes. He cocked his eye up at the pressure-dial. The needle was rock still, not even trembling, a degree or two below a red line painted on the dial.

Brunt continued his tour of the cab. There was a little metal door to a sort of cupboard in the front part of the tender, and he had no reservations about opening it: an oil-can, a spanner, a ball of cotton waste – and tucked away in the back a red-bound book, carefully wrapped round with several layers of white linen. It seemed an unusual possession for a man of the apparent outlook of Thos Beresford: *Under the Eaves* or *The Stolen Golden Hour* by the Author of *The Meek in Spirit*. Brunt lifted the cover and was for a moment bemused by the bookplate: *Awarded to Amy Harrington, 12th September, 1869, for a composition on the Evils of Strong Drink. Signed Jno. Wildebloode, Superintendent, Wesleyan Sunday Schools, Melbourne Street, Tapton, Derbys.*

Brunt dismissed the temptation to slip the book into his own case. It was patience that had earned him his promotion – the ability to sit innocently on acquired knowledge. He carefully wrapped the volume back in its linen and had just pushed it behind the oil-can when the steam-valve blew.

The pressure was prodigious, the noise of it almost beyond toleration. Brunt struggled to remember what Beresford had told him to do. The main water-cock turned easily for him. He heard water pouring down under the cab, hissing against the hot plates. He opened the injector valve a fraction, heard steam escaping along the boiler casing; *get a cone*, Beresford had said. Brunt pushed the valve full open. And nothing happened; water continued to escape somewhere under the locomotive – he had visions of emptying the vital tank. He shut down all the taps and tried starting the process afresh. But there was some knack that he lacked. The steam flow would not take up the water supply.

Then he heard two shots, an interval, and two more. Beresford could not possibly have failed to hear what was happening to his engine; therefore he was not worried by it; therefore he was positively enjoying Brunt's discomfiture: a man with a sense of humour that needed to be watched.

Then suddenly Thos Beresford was hauling himself back into the cab, cursing convincingly. He flung a bundle of lifeless rabbits over the crates on to the coals.

'That's the last bloody time I'll leave you in charge of this engine.'

'Thank God for that.'

Beresford operated the same brass handles that Brunt had, but to proper effect. The safety-valve shut itself off, a heaven of comparative silence. Then the fireman was clambering up into his own corner of the cab, dumping a sack on to the tender. Beresford opened the stiff pilot-valve of the regulator and they lurched forward. The foot-plate swayed as they gathered speed. It was impossible to remain on one's feet without bracing oneself against something in the cab – which meant being blistered against this piece of metal or bruised against that. A wholly hostile machine: yet Beresford seemed to have an affection for the creature that amounted to idolatry. He never touched the spoke of a wheel or the handle of a lever without immediately running a piece of soft, clean rag over it.

Just as Brunt was beginning to find his foot-plate legs, Beresford closed down the main valve and they came smoothly to a stop beside a wooden platform, some twenty feet long, with no station furniture other than a rudimentary shelter. Behind the Halt, on a hill shaped like a sugar-loaf, stood a pile of stones like a truncated cone: *Pedlar's Stump*. Beresford grasped Brunt's wrists in hands of primeval strength and helped him out of the cab.

'You're staying in Piper's Fold, then?'

'I'm hoping I'll get a room at the inn.'

'They'll find you one if you say Thos Beresford sent you.'

But Beresford was making no motion to hand him down his case. Brunt took a step forward and reached up for it.

'We'll be seeing you tonight in the *Rake*,' Beresford said. 'And we come on horse-back. You'd best let us carry it for you.'

It was impossible to know whether the offer was genuinely thoughtful. More likely Beresford was curious to know what this odd-looking character was carrying. It was more than conceivable that he was downright dishonest. And it was unthinkable that Brunt should allow himself to become parted from his burden. It contained confidential police papers – as well as one or two additional small specimens from Isaac Mosley's Ottoman collection. He put a foot on the lowest step of the cab and one hand on the iron hand-rail.

'Don't be so bloody silly,' Beresford said. 'And we haven't all night to be arguing with you. We've got to get this bloody engine back. Shed foreman doesn't know we've got the bugger out.'

Brunt continued to advance up the iron steps and as he did so he saw that in the momentary shock of the steam valve's blowing he had not properly fastened the door of the locker in the tender. In the same instant Thos Beresford, following Brunt's eyes, put two and two together – though whether it was his conclusions that made him lose his temper, Brunt never really knew. He picked up Brunt's bag and flung it far out of the cab, over Brunt's head, over the post and rail fence beyond the platform. It landed heavily on the bank beyond. And the Beresford eyebrows conveyed the impression that Brunt need not look forward to their next meeting.

'You won't be the first traveller to turn up in Piper's Fold with a load too big for him,' Beresford said.

The engine steamed away, and Brunt fumbled with the fastening of the gate that would let him on to the track up Piper's Clough.

Chapter Three

The path up the Clough had been made by and for sheep rather than man. At times it disappeared altogether, apparently following the bed of a stream, at present dried up after the hot summer. The valley reminded Brunt of the parable of the Good Samaritan. It was in just such boulder-strewn desolation that a robber's victim might be left dry-throated and bleeding whilst passers-by attended to their own business. And the appearance of barrenness and neglect was increased by the many trial adits that had been driven into the rock by generations of lead-miners: dark holes surrounded by the great heaps of stone waste that had been torn out of the workings.

Brunt had no doubt that every yard of his progress up the sterile cleft was being watched from behind some rock or other. No stranger came up Piper's Clough without every yard accounted for – and, he reflected, if Amy Harrington had left the village voluntarily, her progress would equally have been public knowledge. Every few minutes he looked back over his shoulder, scanned the waving nettles, the stunted trees, the rain-hollowed rock-shelters. But he saw no man. He met no man in his path. It took him three-quarters of an hour to cover a distance of a mile and a half, up the gradient that was often one in five.

And then he came upon his first view of the village – Piper's Fold: 502 inhabitants, of whom only two were in view as he emerged into the village street: a child in a dirty pinafore, who took flight with no shoes to her feet; and an old woman in a cottage doorway who seemed deaf to his greeting.

He quickly found *The Crooked Rake*, pushed his shoulder against a warped door that jammed after the first few degrees, and eventually forced his way into the bar and out of the nineteenth century. Conversation was suspended, clay pipes and tankards forgotten at the sight of him.

He knew that he had walked in on a scene which differed little from the one which must first have met the eyes of the Turk. The room had pots, tables, benches, uncushioned, high-backed settles, and very little else. And of the group of men who were sitting round the walls, Brunt was prepared to expect anything – except initiative on the side of the law. Centuries of inbreeding had accentuated oddities of feature. Eyes were weak-minded and lacked lustre. The Pennine blizzards had weathered cheekbones to a broken-veined gauntness. Long years of stooping in rough-hewn galleries had bent backs and bowed legs.

Brunt went to the landlord, a shirt-sleeved man called Nadin with a fringe of curls flattened against his forehead, who looked as if he were casting about in his mind for any excuse to refuse him a room. Eventually he accepted him, with the merest of nods.

'And I'll have a slice of whatever joint you have standing on your sideboard,' Brunt said. He bought himself a pint of ale, and after he had been seen to take a mouthful of it in the same way as any other man might, some brave spirit actually spoke to him.

'You'll have had a long walk, then?'

'Might have been longer. I got a lift on a railway engine.'

'So you met Thos Beresford?'

'I did that.'

A murmur of approval. Presumably they felt that if Thos had disapproved of him, he would not be here. Somebody laughed.

'Did he tell you any tales about his rappit?'

'His rappit?'

'Never comes in here of an evening but he tells us a tale about his rappit.'

'Only rappit in the kingdom that's ever been known to fight a dog. He's had to put steel struts into its hutch. Their old tom-cat keeps out of the way when he lets it out.'

'He's taught it to count, you know. Leastways, it can tap with its foot, up to three. Tells him which trap to bet on, when they're racing whippets, over on Moggeridge Top. If he wins, he always takes it a bottle of oatmeal stout home. We've had a fair notion for some time that one of his wives is supping that.'

'Aye, but which one?' somebody asked, and a belt of coarse laughter went round the room.

'Happen Thos'll have too much on his mind for a rappit story today when he hears what the Rector's up to.'

'Well, you can hardly blame the Rector, can you?'

'You'd better try telling that to Thos. Sooner you than me.'

Some local *cause célèbre*, no doubt. Brunt began to differentiate between the various speakers. Some were clearly fonder of Thos than others. One little man with lips falling in to toothless gums had fighting confidence in him.

'Thos will settle him this time, you'll see. Thos has got time for all sorts of things since he lost his little playmate.'

Then followed a silence of ghastly embarrassment, the company as a whole realising that, whatever this referred to, it was going too far in the presence of a stranger. The man who had made the remark tried to cover it up with pathetic self-justification.

'Well, you know what I mean, Sammy.'

'Aye, we know what you mean. Better not let Thos hear you talk about it, that's all.'

And this silenced the little man with shattering effect. Presumably he could picture all too vividly how Thos might react. A moment or two later they were interrupted by a maid-servant who brought in Brunt's supper: a big girl, bursting with healthy young womanhood, yet somehow, it seemed, nervous to be serving him. She had large hands that fumbled with the chutney jar, liquid eyes that seemed reluctant to meet his own. As if to keep her spirits up as she moved about his table, she was humming unbecomingly to herself: some simple tune that he had heard somewhere before, but to which he could not give a name.

A plate of cold beef and half a loaf of home-baked bread, a trencher-board of crumbling Cheshire cheese to follow. She was relieved to have unloaded her tray, anxious to back away from him. But he was not going to allow her to escape as easily as that.

'And what's your name?'

'Mildred, sir.'

She had a turn of speech that was restfully melodic, a contrast to the stone-wall vowels of the men in the room.

'You're not from these parts?'

'From Bristol, sir.'

Yes, that was it, the West Country: the sort of tavern-wench who might have waited on Amyas Leigh – or on Captain Flint's crew. So people came into the High Peak from the outside world, did they?

'You're a long way from home, Mildred.'

'Yes, sir.'

She was waiting now, obedient – but intensely anxious to be dismissed.

'And you're sure your name's Mildred? It isn't, for example, Amy?'

Absurd, on the face of it, but effective nevertheless. Brunt saw the blood flush her cheeks, was aware of the increase in her pulse-rate, saw that her fingers were tight on the edge of the tray. And the tension was equally palpable throughout the room. Men stopped talking amongst themselves. All eyes were turned inward towards Brunt. He looked unconcernedly round their faces as he silently munched his food. Suspicion, empty mirth, quick anger, vindictiveness, shrewd wisdom, herd stupidity: all were there in ravelled intermixture and above all else, the ability to stand together and hold their tongues for some point of ancient and inarticulate principle.

Brunt ate his meal at drawn-out leisure, then went up to the counter, set down his tankard under the landlord's nose, feeling in his waistcoat pocket for the five-piastre piece. The sight of that might loosen their tongues – or lock their jaws for evermore.

Nadin stooped to the bung and Brunt waited. Then the landlord stood up and set the tankard down, foam overflowing. He took the coin between his thumb and forefinger and held it up to examine it. Brunt could not easily analyse the nature of his reaction. It was not fear; it was not anger; it was not indignation. His eyes were steady, his thin lips tight. He was looking at Brunt with a sort of resentful accusation – resignation, perhaps to the fact that the curtain was up on some final act, though God knows what had gone before.

But the moment was not allowed to develop. There was a diversion, a rattle of hooves in the yard, and a voice that Brunt already knew, one accustomed to making itself heard above the maelstrom of steam, smoke and heaving cylinders.

'Get up there, blast thy axle-box!'

'That's his horse,' somebody said unnecessarily. 'Old Nought-Four-Nought.' Then Beresford came into the room followed by the fireman with the enormous head. The awkward front door offered them no difficulty, opening on its hinges easily enough for them. Brunt's suit-case was still just within it, and Beresford kicked it casually with the side of his foot as he passed it. There was nothing vicious in the gesture – one might almost call it affectionate, as if a symbolic grievance was now paid off. But Beresford came straight up to Brunt and took the coin from his fingers, spun it once in the air, caught it in his capricious palm and handed it back, craggy knuckles uppermost.

'Don't bring it out in here again.'

This instruction was underlined by a single spasmodic motion up and down of the eloquent brows. Beresford then turned his back on Brunt and lowered his first pint in a draught. The fireman, Jack Plant, was only a fraction of a second behind his mentor.

'Well, Thos, and what's thy rappit been up to today?'

Beresford turned to face his questioner, embarked on an anecdote that he had clearly been preparing all day.

'Well, I reckon we must have had somebody up to no good in the Fold last night – a prowler. Anyway, I heard the hutch door open – he's learnt to open it for himself, you know. There was a bit of a scuffle, and I thought I heard footsteps making off. I don't know what really happened, but the old rappit had blood on its whiskers when I took him his breakfast this morning.'

There was some laughter, but it fell short of hilarity. An awkward silence followed. Beresford slewed round to look insolently for the effect of the story on Brunt. Then he came slowly across the room, put his hand in the vast poacher's pocket inside his jacket.

'I think you'll have an interest in this, mister.'

It was Amy Harrington's red-backed novel, still wrapped in the white linen in which Brunt had first seen it. He put it down on the table without looking at it, but made no attempt to deny that he had seen it before.

'Found?' he asked.

'She must have left it on a bench in the waiting-room at Cromford Wharf, the day she left – oh, months ago. I've been waiting to hand it to someone with authority – with real authority, I mean.'

Brunt had not announced any authority, but Beresford was an intelligent observer.

'She was on your train, Mr Beresford?'

'I was on shunting duties, higher up the line, that morning.'

'But somebody must have seen her go.'

'Nobody saw her go. I found her book, that's all. Perhaps because I was meant to.'

'There are questions I need to ask.'

'I know nothing, mister. None of us knows anything. If you want to know more than nothing, you'll have to ask Kingsey.'

He went back to where he had left his pot. Some man in the company delivered them from embarrassment.

'Have you seen the Parish Magazine, Thos?'

'It was laid out open on the table for me when I got home.'

'*All those who are not in full communion—*' There was some attempt at ecclesiastical mimicry, but not very successful, because the speaker's native vowels were too strong to be suppressed, '*are henceforward to be debarred from holding Rectory allotments.*'

'He can't take land off a man that still bears a crop that he's planted. That's common law.'

'How long have you dug that patch, Thos?'

'Twenty-five years. The Rector let me keep it when he first came here. Happen he thought he might get me to church that way.

Mind you, I was always disqualified from winning any Festival Prize.'

'So what will you do when you've dug your taters, Thos? Get something else planted overnight?'

'I'll think of something.'

He filled the bowl of a clay pipe with finely shredded shag.

'Happen the Rector will have to go the same way as Kingsey,' he said at last.

'But that's not going to settle much, is it?' said a little man called Sammy Nall who, Brunt had already noticed, seemed less under Beresford's thumb than the others.

'Happen not. But it'll be good for a laugh.'

Then conversation was muted as a comparative stranger came in through the front door – someone they all knew, but clearly a class apart from them: a middle-aged man still striving after youth – black trousers, slim fitting; clean shaven about the chin, but with a line of waxed tip moustache; sideboards sharply clipped to the bottom of his lobes; shinily pomaded hair. Unselfcritical vanity; Brunt guessed that he was one of Kingsey's entourage. Footman probably; perhaps one of the few from the Hall who had much contact with the world outside. Not many from below stairs would often come in here.

But a few minutes later another from the same quarters came in. The butler, this one, obviously – braided black trousers showing below his greatcoat; a pompous man with white mutton-chop whiskers; accustomed to command, but knowing better than to try to be imperious in here, though he clearly expected – and got – a certain showing of respect. He had busy eyes, but Brunt thought that he was probably not very sharp-witted. He was carrying, incongruously with his rig, a canvas bag from which Nadin drew a quart-size flagon. And the butler drank a single pint whilst this was being filled at the tap of the barrel. Then he put on his hat, picked up his bag, wished the company a portentous goodnight and left. It stood out forcibly that he and the footman had not acknowledged each other's presence.

Brunt knew that some of his colleagues would not have dragged themselves away from that tap-room whilst there was a midnight toper still talking. But Brunt was a patient man. It suited him to let people's attitudes develop at their own pace, and he knew they were more likely to do so behind his back. He had often heard his grandmother say that you did not open an oven door whilst a Yorkshire pudding was still rising. Moreover, he was physically tired, and asked early for his candle.

For a while he lay in the darkness and tried to think of a line of questioning for Captain Kingsey tomorrow. And what kind of captain? Brunt knew not the first thing about him. A sea captain? A captain of Dragoons? Hussars? Infantry of the line? And why, if the man had any substance behind him at all, should he isolate himself in a hole like Piper's Fold?

Brunt became aware that someone was moving about in the passage outside his bedroom: a step first this way and then that; the creak of a floor-board here by the door, then there further along the wall. He strained his ears. There were other sounds in the night that interfered agonisingly with hearing: a dog, distressed, in someone's yard; a chimney cowl, squealing on the turn. But then in a pause he heard someone humming; and now he remembered the name of the tune. *The Banks of Sacramento*: a ditty that would not have sounded out of place on the West Country waterfront.

Brunt lit his candle and girdled on his dressing-gown. Treading quietly, he thrust open his bedroom door suddenly. There was a candle on the landing, standing on the floor, and the girl was standing in front of the open doors of a colossus of a linen cupboard.

'Trying to get ahead of myself and save myself work for tomorrow.'

This time she did allow her emotional brown eyes to rest on him. Her basket was standing some way away from her, and he guessed that she was only making a pretence of sorting out the stacks of sheets and pillow-cases. His first thought was that she might have come up here to offer herself for a price, which might or might not accord with her nervousness of him while she was serving him at table. Or perhaps she was under orders to come up and offer herself, with or without a price. He made a slight movement towards her that he intended her to interpret as lustful, and she took a step away from him in a manner that he did not think was merely coquettish. Nor did he think that it showed her to be a practised hand.

So it was for some other purpose that she was idling about on the landing: because she wanted to talk to him – or wanted him to talk to her? She was frightened of him, yet she was here, in the hope of seeing him. Bemused by the very thing she dreaded, the ancient case of the rabbit and the snake?

'Why are you afraid of me?' he asked her gently.

'I'm not afraid – sir.'

'No? How old are you, Mildred?'

'Nineteen, sir.'

She was holding his eyes steadily.

'And someone has told you that they think I am a policeman? So you are afraid that I will have you carried back to Bristol?'

'I wouldn't be afraid of going back to Bristol, sir.'

'No? Where did you work, then, when you first left Bristol?'

'In Gloucester, sir.'

She was still looking at him unflickering, but struggling not to drop her eyes.

'So how do you come to be working at *The Crooked Rake*?'

'I was at the Hall, sir, at Captain Kingsey's.'

'And you ran away from there? As you ran away from Gloucester?'

She was silent.

'How long ago, Mildred? When did you come to this inn?'

'About a year ago, sir.'

She was attractive. Brunt could not know for certain how firm or easy her morals might be, but he felt sure that the roots of her present fear were not in sex.

'So it was when you left – *because* you left – that Amy Harrington came?'

The very mention of the name struck ice into her. For seconds he allowed the flickering candle-light, the angular shadows of the open cupboard doors, to play on her imagination. He shifted one foot a sudden inch and she jumped. He lifted his stubby fingers slowly to his uncouth chin. She thought he was going to reach out for her with his hand, and she cringed.

'So why did you run away from Captain Kingsey?'

'Sir – leave me alone!'

'I haven't touched you, Mildred. I'm not going to touch you. I am talking to you because you have come up here to tell me something.'

'No, sir.'

'About Amy Harrington.'

'*No*, sir. Sir, Amy Harrington's gone away . . . of her own accord . . .'

'Is that what someone has told you to tell me?'

He stood staring at her, making capital out of his repulsive looks. He had broken more than one case on men's stupefaction by his ugliness.

'Did anyone see her go? That's what I need to know.'

Downstairs someone opened a door, but took only a step or two, as if straining ears to know what was being said above. The girl suddenly twisted on her heel in front of him, abandoned her candle but seized the handle of her empty basket and fled with it down the corridor. He heard her stumbling on the lower stairs and struggling with the door into the kitchen quarters. Brunt carefully closed the door of the linen cupboard.

Of course, a good deal of what the Chief Constable had said remained nonsense. But Brunt knew now that he had not been sent up to Piper's Fold for nothing.

Chapter Four

Brunt lay back on the bed, the candle still fluttering, and gazed up at the wandering geography of the ceiling. The girl Mildred had put some new possibilities about Amy Harrington into his mind.

If Eleanor Copley had done nothing else for Amy Harrington, she had produced for her the first room, the first bed even, in which she had ever slept alone. Brunt had a vivid picture of what life must have been like for a child in the Harrington home: the fire-and-sword discipline of the dissenting churches, translated into a razor-strop across the buttocks for trivial infringements. The domestic rages; the nightly stinking ritual when her father pissed the fire out; the animal sexual bouts that rocked the slum; the devolution of her mother – the sudden inexplicable withdrawal, perhaps to the accompaniment of an unexplained back-hander across the mouth, of the caresses that had stopped when she ceased to be a babe in arms. Yet they had continued the struggle of those weekly letters, the vital importance of the simnel cake. Ritual. Superstition.

And had Amy Harrington been a dreamer? About what? About some reward for constancy of the sort that happened in the closing chapter of a Sunday School prize? Often that amounted to nothing more lascivious than a sadly happy death between unaccustomed clean, cool sheets. Or, somewhere or other, had Amy Harrington caught a glimpse of what she took to be life? In the big house to which she had gone at Rowsley, perhaps? Brunt had seen extraordinary developments when some of these kids moved to the edge of another world.

So why had she come to Piper's Fold from Rowsley? Why had

the other girl come here from Gloucester? Was there a common pattern? Two girls – one of them, at least, who had in abundance what most men wanted. She had escaped – if you could call *The Crooked Rake* an escape. And the other?

Mildred served him his breakfast in the morning, lethargic but polite, her eyes averted, making no reference at all to their meeting on the landing. Behind Brunt's back the door of the kitchen was ajar, someone moving about behind it in desultory fashion, keeping within hearing distance. Not until he had finished his second cup of tea, and the girl was impatient to clear the table, did Brunt speak to her.

'I need to know your full name. Also the address of your parents, and of the place at which you worked in Gloucester.'

'Mildred Jarman, sir.'

It was a whisper, meekly compliant, but with an air of resignation, as if she were surrendering all that she still had to live for.

'It'll make things easier for us both, if you'll tell me what I'm sure to find out in Gloucester.'

'You can take me back to Gloucester if you like,' she said, with unconvincing defiance, the west coast burr more marked than ever.

'Mildred, last night you were on the landing because you wanted to tell me something.'

'No, sir.'

'You don't have to tell me this very minute.' He looked significantly towards the kitchen door. 'But any time you feel you'd like to. I frightened you last night, and that was stupid of me. I'm here to find out what happened to Amy Harrington – and to make sure it happens to no one else.'

'There is nothing I can tell you, sir.'

And within the kitchen someone took a single step on the stone flagged floor, a reminder to her. Brunt got up, pushed the door open and came upon Nadin, the landlord, standing with a pan inanely in one hand, neither coming nor going.

'You'd be better occupied, Nadin, in helping me to get things squared up.'

'All I know is, I want no trouble.'

'It seems to me you're not going to have much choice about that.'

Brunt let himself into the village street, surprisingly warm and fresh after the sour beer and inert tobacco fumes of the inn. He fingered the five-piastre piece, strangely a comfort to him. He called first on the old woman who, through deafness or otherwise, had failed to return his greeting when he had first walked into the village. He was not quite certain why he chose her for a visit, except that she had struck him with an air of detached, impoverished dignity which appealed to him. She would almost certainly have no connections with *The Crooked Rake* set and had looked as if she might be sufficiently lonely to be aloof from village opinion.

The cottage was humble – for once the adjective was apposite – but he could not help being impressed by the quality of three or four pieces of glassware which she had on a small shelf evidently put up for this single purpose. And she *was* deaf. Brunt found himself shouting, simplifying, repeating. He put the Turkish coin into her hand.

'Have you ever seen one like this before?'

She went straight to a curtained alcove and brought out the twin of it, which she thrust at him.

'Here, take it. Given to me by my mother, and to her by hers. And it's brought none of us anything but misery. A shameful story, a disgrace to the whole village. And I suppose I'm in trouble with you, now, for having it in the house?'

'No, nothing like that,' Brunt said, and tried to put her at her ease. He could turn on a decent smile when he wanted to. 'But there are other things that are a disgrace to this village, aren't there? I said *other things* – disgrace to the village—'

'I can follow you better if you talk quietly,' she said. Of course, lip-reading. Brunt was ashamed of himself for not having thought of it.

'I said, there are other things that go on in this village . . .'

She screwed up her face with disgust. 'Artists and painters . . .'

'You mean at the Hall. Does Captain Kingsey give big parties?'

She shook her head. 'It's a small mercy that he keeps himself very closely to himself. But that doesn't help those who are close tied to him.'

'What sort of goings-on?' Brunt asked.

'Disgusting.'

Brunt wanted to ask her how she knew, but she could not have given him an articulate answer. Moreover, Brunt understood: there was such a thing as community consciousness. No one had stopped to analyse what had happened to the Turkish pedlar; no one had dared to talk about it; but everyone had known.

'Take that slip of a girl, the one that ran away. If you ask me, she was the lucky one.'

'Amy Harrington, you mean?'

'I don't know what they called her. I only know she didn't stay. Though it's true that no one saw the going of her.'

'No one?'

'They say. They say she got away. But it's funny, no one will speak to having seen her. No one saw her down the Clough. No one can speak to having seen her on the Fly.'

'Who are *they*, Mrs Hallum?'

But he knew that it was a useless question.

'People,' she said. 'You can't hide things from people.'

Brunt's next call was at the Beresfords' cottage, having first assured himself that at this hour Thos was himself either driving his train or shooting rabbits somewhere on the long stretch between the Bunsall and the Hopton Inclines.

There were several striking things about Thos's home. The first was that the diamond-slatted trellis-work on which a few late roses climbed beside the porch was of precisely the same vintage as adorned one or two of the C. and H.P's prouder stations. In place of a door-knob there was a four-spoked brass wheel of the kind with which Brunt had yesterday failed to operate an injector. He paused before knocking at the door, for a quarrel was going on inside the house, producing as much noise, it seemed, as half a street in Tapton or Ilkeston could have created. And yet there were only two voices raised in heathen dissonance. The subject of contention seemed to be someone's head, and it seemed – as far as any running sense at all could be made of the argument – that this member had become detached and that what was at issue was the extent and nature of surgery required. Brunt rapped with his knuckles and the quarrel was silenced in mid-syllable. A cat came up and began rubbing itself against Brunt's ankle, no doubt intending to slip into the house under cover of his entrance.

Judging that the inmates may not have been certain of his first knock, Brunt rapped again, and this time the door was opened to him by two women who stood looking at him from a yard or two apart: one of them a chubby little baked apple of a woman with an inverted Cupid's bow of a mouth that gave the impression she was always smiling; the other grotesquely tall, with a face whose ferocity, if assumed, must make her one of the finest actresses in the land.

'I'd like to speak to Mrs Beresford,' Brunt said.

'Oh, yes? Which one?'

'Mrs Thos Beresford.'

The tall one stood aside with a mock heroic sweep of her forearm.

'Come in,' she said, 'and take your pick.'

Chapter Five

Thos Beresford had not been content with taking two wives. Perhaps it was understandable that no ordinary woman would have been adequate for him; but even in duplication he appeared to have achieved something over the odds. The interior of the cottage was in a state of chaos doubtless reflecting the underlying philosophies of the household.

'Actually, we are sisters,' the taller one explained. '*And* good friends.'

'I expect you need to be,' Brunt said, 'if you're both married to Thos.'

'I can assure you, Mr Brunt, *that* was done in a church.'

Indeed? In the absence presumably of officiating clergy. The ogress allowed her lower lip to sag, revealing irregular yellow teeth in the basic intention of a smile. Within the course of the next few minutes Brunt concluded that the chubby one's smile was wholly illusory and the other one's scowl equally misleading. No doubt Thos had come to terms with it.

'I said to Lois, that gentleman from the detective office will be dropping in, didn't I, Lois?'

'You did, Dora.'

Lois smiled, or didn't smile, as the case might be. Brunt allowed his eyes to begin a scientific exploration of the room. He eventually decided that what the two women were engaged upon was a preliminary skirmish for a sewing operation. Like some soldiers, who will not attack until they have established their supporting forces, the Beresford women evidently believed in getting ready first. They were stylists; they thought big; when they sewed, it was on a grand scale. Wools, cottons, thimbles – two lidless boxes of them – mushrooms, embroidery frames: everything they had seemed to have been got out in preparation.

Moreover, it was not immediately clear what genre of workmanship was being contemplated. Perhaps running repairs were about to be broached to some of Thos's old clothes, for these lay about the room in great profusion: boiler-suits, trousers, hats, socks and even boots. But if this were the case, then it looked as if half a life-time's accumulated deficiencies were about to be put right for the remainder of Thos's days. Dora pioneered a route across the room for him by seizing an armful of assorted rags and throwing them up into the air. Brunt, picking up a pair of long woollen underpants, and dropping them as respectfully as he could on a corner of the fender, made himself a space on which he sat. He then brought the coin out of his pocket and passed it over to Lois.

'Beresford has got a lot of those,' Dora said. 'But then, if he isn't entitled to them, who is? The ostler was his direct ancestor, and he paid the price.'

'Price.' The other one invariably came in late with the last word or two of her sister's speech.

'So what Beresford has, has, as you might say, been paid for.'

'For.'

Brunt leaped from his chair and extracted an errant needle from his bottom.

'Tell me, ladies, has Beresford to your knowledge ever tried to sell any of his collection?'

'Oh, no. He'd never do that.'

'That.'

'You're sure?'

Dora was; she nodded violently. But Lois was not so certain. Brunt watched suspicion cloud her eyes, though it still did not detract from the misleading merriment of her mouth. After a moment of unconcealed mental unease she brought out a tin box whose lid bore a scene from Gainsborough. She plunged in both hands, as if she were about to bring out a lump of dough, producing instead two handsful of mixed coin from various empires. Her sister cleared a corner of the table and for silent minutes she sorted the money out into regular piles, appearing to know her way well about the denominations. At one point she appeared puzzled and anxious, as if something was not in order, and at this moment there was no sound in their room but their breathing and the ticking of a clock.

At the beginning of his visit, Brunt had been struck by a powerful and bewildering feeling of unreality – as if he had walked out of Derbyshire into the middle of a Punch and Judy show. But of a sudden these two improbable women were immersed in something that was vital to them, Dora intently watching her sister's every move. Lois suddenly found a fugitive small coin that had become sandwiched between two larger neighbours. Brunt almost shared their relief.

'It's all there.'

'Of course,' Brunt said. 'There must be similar collections in the village.'

'Not many, nowadays. A lot got lost, some was sold. Though, of course, when all's said and done. Captain Kingsey has the lion's share. It stands to sense.'

'Does it?' Brunt asked.

'Naturally. If you look at the list of vicars' names in the church, you'll see the Reverend Jeremiah Kingsey, 1706 to 1723. Actually, the Captain is only a very distant relation. The Hall came to him through a distant cousin when the line ran out. And all that was in it.'

'You're not suggesting that even the vicar was involved in that business?'

'Good gracious, no. Vicars don't go mixing themselves up in that sort of caper. But the Reverend Kingsey, you see, he was the chief one of the magistrates, when they had the trial in *The Crooked Rake*. He always was as thick as thieves with the landlord.'

Dora gave what was meant to be an affectionate kick at the mountain of old clothes, sending several garments flying through the air at shoulder level.

'That's what this lot is for, the Rector – the present one, of course.'

'Really?'

'Because we're going to burn him at the stake.'

'Indeed?'

'In effigy, you know. Because he has thrown Beresford off his allotment.'

'And do you think that will make him change his mind?'

'It did once before, years ago, when he was a young man and tried to stop the gravediggers from drinking beer.'

'I see.'

But Brunt had just seen something else, thrown to the top of the pile by Dora's ecstatic kick. He leaned forward and picked it up: a girl's cheap cape in black cashmere. On the underside of the lower hem, worked in not very elegant stitches, were the initials *A.H.* Brunt looked up and saw that both women's eyes were motionless on him.

'I can see you looking at that,' Dora said.

'Does that surprise you?'

'*That* came from the Hall, from Captain Kingsey, amongst a lot of stuff he sent out to the jumble sale. I expect it belonged to that young lady who ran away.'

'I expect it did.'

'And who's to blame her for that? For running away, I mean. The things that people say go on at that Hall. You ought to talk to Beresford about it.'

'I probably will.'

'He can tell you a lot about the Hall, can Beresford. And about Amy Harrington.'

'I dare say he can.'

At which moment Dora accidentally caught a delicately poised box in a dramatic sweep of her arm, showering Brunt in an enfilading fire of thimbles. As he left the house, he heard the quarrel start up again.

Chapter Six

Brunt was received at the Hall with scrupulous courtesy but with equally deliberate lack of warmth. Edwards, the butler, whom he had observed the previous evening buying his ale for consumption off the premises, had the art of observing social forms whilst at the same time making it plain that his own judgment was reserved – and might, indeed, never be expressed. He kept his eye dutifully averted from Brunt's dress, though it was clear that such lack of pride would never be tolerated below stairs – except perhaps in an under-gardener in inclement weather.

Captain Kingsey looked a younger man than Brunt had been expecting. He looked barely into his forties, though his jowls were beginning to fill out. He was wearing a dark blue smoking-jacket with quilted lapels, held at the waist by a girdle of red silken rope. On his head he had a soft round pill-box hat, embroidered with some oriental motif that Brunt could not interpret, and from the centre of its crown a red tassel hung rakishly down to his left ear. The impression that his manner gave was subtle but not unclear: he was not positively offended by Brunt's visit, but not amused by it, either; nor was he persuaded that it was likely to serve any useful purpose. He was prepared to unbend sufficiently to answer any reasonable questions, but his interpretation of what was reasonable was likely to be circumscribed and uncompromising.

He walked with a halt in his left foot, barely perceptible but inescapable – there was evidence about his souvenirs that he had been an army man. He led Brunt along the polished parquet of a long corridor with alcoves lined with paintings, mostly in oils and of landscapes. And he maintained a commentary, marked by a certain weary glibness, as he watched where Brunt's eyes were lingering.

'Joseph Stannard, of the Norwich School: *The Maltings, Stoke-by-Nayland*; Hayman: Study for a scene from *Clarissa Harlowe*; ah, and I see, Sergeant, that you are a man of some artistic discernment. What you are looking at there is one of Cotman's original sketches for Dawson Turner's *Architectural Antiquities of Normandy*.'

He took Brunt to a large, quiet study on an upper floor, the walls lined with bindings some of which were as old as the printed book.

'Now, Sergeant, you have not come here to consider *objets d'art*.'

'Not indeed for their intrinsic merits, that is true, sir, though they may not be entirely irrelevant. There are in fact two issues that I am trying to resolve, and they may be inter-related.'

Kingsey had coffee brought for himself in a Sèvres service, and lit himself a cigar from a box labelled *Villar y Villar*. He offered Brunt no hospitality.

'Two things, sir. Firstly, the disappearance of a seventeen-year-old housemaid, by name Amy Harrington. Secondly, the possible theft of a number of articles, principally coins of various realms, but predominantly of Near Eastern provenance.'

Kingsey smiled thinly and got up from his desk.

'Possibly inter-related, I think you said, Sergeant?'

He went to a redwood cabinet, pulled open a shallow drawer and showed Brunt a numismatologist's tray with hand-written labels still gummed beneath its empty round slots.

'Possibly inter-related? The absence of the girl and of these coins was noticed on precisely the same morning, to wit the twenty-third of April last. I began at the time to make an inventory of what was missing: it became such a bore that I never finished it. There were two engine-tooled ornamental candlesticks, virtually valueless, but of a certain vulgar intricacy that might have misled a house-maid. There was a square of Caucasian tapestry that really is unique.'

'At least, sir, we think that we may have recovered some of your treasures. Almost certainly some of the coins; and I have no doubt you can identify the tapestry?'

Kingsey looked pleasantly interested, but by no means excited.

'And when do you think, Sergeant, that I might regain possession?'

'There will have to be formalities, of course, to establish your ownership. A line or two of affidavit will suffice. But we cannot help wondering why you did not report your losses.'

Kingsey smiled pathetically. 'Sergeant Brunt, you will have noticed that I live in a lonely, one might almost say a desolate spot – and I am here wholly by choice. I claim to be a happy man. I am surrounded by what I like and I spend the whole of my time doing the things that I want to. I do not have to worry where my next cigar – or, for that matter, my next square of Caucasian tapestry – is to come from. That last one cost a large sum of money – but peace, freedom from interruption, freedom to get on with my critical history of English painting – these things are priceless to me, too.'

His smile became decidedly rueful.

'Nevertheless,' Brunt said, 'we cannot expect to control the criminal classes if the public will not take us into their confidence.'

'No, of course, I see that. I seem to have failed signally as a dutiful citizen. But I cannot bring myself to think of my departed house-maid as a menace to society. An opportunist, perhaps; a stupid girl. She may have acted in panic because of something that she misunderstood.'

Brunt was bright with interest. 'What sort of thing had you in mind, sir?'

'I had nothing in mind at all, Sergeant. I don't know what goes on in their silly little brains.'

'If I may remind you, sir, you did tell the girl's father, when you answered his letter, that you would lay charges against her if she should endeavour to return.'

'Did I? I must take your word for it, I cannot remember. I regard consistency as an unnecessary bore; but that is a luxury such as you could hardly allow yourself in the lower reaches of your police force. I wanted to make it clear that I had no wish for her to come importuning me in an access of remorse.'

'You think she was the sort of girl who might do so?'

'I really could not say, Sergeant.'

'Forgive me, sir, but I do not fully understand. You said just now that she might have endeavoured to come back. I cannot quite see why you should have expected that.'

'I did not expect it, Sergeant. I thought it was on the cards that she might have tried. And that would have irritated me beyond toleration. I have a horror of hysteria. These girls have some stupid notions: sententious moral ideas, derived from the silly novels that they read by candlelight. Faced by her first set-backs in the outside world, she might have returned with her loot to snivel for forgiveness. Such a scene could have thrown me off my working aplomb – perhaps for a month.'

'And you considered her the sort of girl from whom to expect such behaviour?'

Kingsey pushed his chair back from his desk. 'Sergeant, what did you say her name was?'

'Amy Harrington, sir.' Brunt answered him with pleasant patience.

'I would be hard pressed, Sergeant, to put a face to the name. A girl like this – like this Amy Harrington – is engaged to light fires and keep the house clean. I do expect certain standards of personal acceptability, but my conception of these is negative rather than positive. The highest demand I make of my servants is that they should not be noticeable. I certainly do not hire them so that I can explore the labyrinthine culs-de-sac of their souls.'

'They do have souls,' Brunt murmured, almost inaudibly, and Kingsey picked it up as smartly as he might at one time have snapped at a piece of insolence on the parade ground.

'What was that, Sergeant?'

'I was merely considering, sir, how often these girls in domestic service do harbour their little illusions.'

'You may be right, Sergeant. For my part, I do not allow it to obtrude on my life. And now it seems to me that the morning is advancing. If you would, as expeditiously as possible, arrange for my property to be brought along here, I will formally identify it.

And if the girl is found, I will contentedly accept your advice about preferring charges.'

But Brunt was not ready to go yet.

'From what I have so far been able to put together about Amy Harrington, I would hardly expect her to have access to a professional fence – indeed, even to know of the existence of such men.'

'An opportunist, Sergeant, as I have already suggested.'

'The man in question was no amateur. He would certainly not buy from a thief he did not know.'

'What are you insinuating?'

'That she had an accomplice. She might even have sought employment here with a view to long-term mischief, though I regard this as extremely unlikely. But if she had been contacted after her arrival here – by someone in the village . . .'

'Sergeant, the village palpably bristles with crime, but essentially of a barbaric and niggardly character. There is no sophistication in Piper's Fold.'

'And amongst your own household staff?' Brunt continued.

'Unthinkable,' Kingsey said.

'Sir, I am sure you are right. But it is something which I hope formally to establish.'

'*I* shall establish it, Sergeant, and it will not take me long.'

'If, sir, I may have your authority to question . . .'

'You will not question any of my servants, Sergeant. And certainly you will not do so behind my back. I shall conduct such questioning as needs to be done myself.'

He tugged the bell-cord and ordered the butler to bring a number of servants to the study.

'Evans and Bootherstone, Mrs Palfreyman, Emma, Elizabeth and Swarbrick.' At least there were some females about the house whose names he seemed to know.

Presently a self-conscious line was standing along the edge of the study carpet, almost to attention. To the right was Edwards, glancing sideways at the straightness of the file. Beside him was Mrs Palfreyman, the housekeeper, a greying, dignified and potentially indignant woman. Next to her was a comfortable looking cook, her fresh red hands washed clean of flour, which nevertheless dusted the lower part of her arms. Then two men-servants, one in a green baize apron. Next two young girls in conventional indoor servants' dress. And finally a kitchen and boot-boy, whose collar was askew and one boot-lace dangling.

'This is your entire household?' Brunt asked.

'I have gardeners; and two labourers, at present mending pot-holes in the estate road. They can be sent for if you wish; but it would take the rest of the morning to get them all here. And it would be less likely even than our present occupation to serve any useful purpose.'

'I was thinking that you had another footman.'

Brunt briefly described the character with the pomaded hair whom he had seen in *The Crooked Rake*; and whom the butler on that occasion had refused to recognise. It was the butler who came to the rescue.

'Fletcher, sir.'

He addressed this remark to his master, pointedly not to Brunt, and that without moving his head or eyes. Kingsey laughed; and this time decidedly unpleasantly.

'There must be something radically amiss with your powers of detection, Sergeant. I do not know what Fletcher would say if he knew you had mistaken him for a footman. He is my agent, Sergeant. I have a London house, which I use only occasionally. A *pied à terre*, no more, and one whose pleasures I forgo with something less exhausting than fortitude. Fletcher is my steward and liaison officer. He left this morning by the Staffordshire Road and the London and North Western Railway. And now.'

He addressed himself to the silent platoon.

'Mr Brunt is a sergeant from the detective division of the County Constabulary. He wishes to put some questions to you. I may say in advance that none of you stands under any kind of suspicion. You may carry on, Sergeant.'

He was hoping, no doubt, to draw Brunt's sting by the sheer starch of ceremony. But Brunt behaved as if nothing could affect his state of relaxation. Ignoring the butler and the housekeeper, he moved down the line to the cook, who looked as if she might be the most amenable of the bunch.

'Tell me what happened on the last night that Amy Harrington spent in this house.'

'There's nothing I can tell you, sir. She was here that night as usual. The next morning we heard that she had gone.'

'At what time was that discovered?'

'As I was cooking the breakfast.'

'And the previous evening? She had seemed normal enough?'

The others were breathing evenly and quietly. Brunt was struck by the quality of the clothes that some of the women were wearing: not so much by the cut of the cloth as by the material itself. He thought that the housekeeper could have passed herself off as the mistress of the house, though the sobriety of the tones she was wearing might have saved her from the suspicion that she was deliberately trying to do so. The housemaid, Emma, appeared to be wearing black silk, rather than the common hard-wearing rep of her kind, and the lace trimmings of her apron, cuffs and collars were surely too fine to stand up to her normal working day.

Brunt looked into the cook's face.

'Come; did she seem worried at all?'

'I can't say that I knew the girl very well – not to understand her, that is. She was a child who mooned about a lot. I'd say that in her last few days she was even moodier than usual.'

Silence from the rest of them. The other two girls, Emma and Elizabeth, were probably exercising every last effort of will-power to try to stop Brunt from catching their eyes.

'You'd say that she was a dreamer, would you?'

'She was often lost in her own thoughts.'

Brunt moved back along the line and faced the housekeeper.

'Would *you* say that she was a dreamer?'

'That's what I would call her.'

'And what sort of thing was she dreaming about, Mrs Palfreyman?'

'I am not a mind-reader, Sergeant.'

Brunt moved down to the younger girls, his idle gait deliberately out of keeping with the military charade.

'Did she ever tell either of you two what she was dreaming about?'

Emma did not speak; but her companion blurted something out.

'She was a bit simple, sir.'

'How, simple?'

'Sir, I don't mean that she was soft in the head, sir. She was – well, sir – she did not always know how to go on in a big house. She didn't like being here.'

'Because you teased her?'

'We used to, a bit, sir, but we meant no harm.'

Then the boot-boy interrupted. 'Sir, when she wasn't on duty, she used to go across a lot to Brindley's Quarter.'

'Brindley's Quarter?'

'She mooned about there, sir. She'd be there on her own for an hour or two at a time.'

'And what and where is Brindley's Quarter?'

Which gave Kingsey his opportunity to take fresh command of the dialogue. 'Obviously, Sergeant, you are not well acquainted with the vocabulary of the lead-mining fraternity.'

'I am more at home with the terminology of the coalface.'

'Yes; you look as if you might be.'

Whereupon the butler actually chuckled.

'Sergeant, I do believe you actually think that a crooked rake is a broken agricultural tool.'

The housekeeper was now smiling broadly.

'I was well aware, sir, that a rake is the main seam of ore in a locality.'

'Brindley was a seventeenth-century optimist who tried to drill into the rake at a point where it had already petered out. A Quarter Cord, Sergeant, is the name given to the space which a stake-holder was allowed round the entrance to his adit, to deposit his waste, to erect a shed for his tools and to accommodate his *buddle*. That is a stone trough used for washing ore.'

'I am obliged to you for the information, sir.'

Was Kingsey merely trying to deter him from questioning the boy?

'But I was unaware that our late-lamented Amy – what was her other name?'

'Harrington, sir.'

'That Amy Harrington had formed the habit of communing at Brindley's Quarter. I am beginning to remember the girl now – now that she has been called a dreamer. She was certainly that. One morning I discovered in the nick of time that she had laid the breakfast-room fire with, among other things, one of my newest Grecian slippers.'

Laughter now the length of the line. Kingsey drew continued cheerfulness from it.

'Brindley's Quarter. Obviously, the Quarter accorded to one Brindley. Well, I fear that Amy Harrington would find little there in the way of an oracle to interpret her dreams for her. Unless, of course, she knew how to call on the Old Man. Does *he* mean anything to you, Sergeant?'

'The Old Man?'

'A composite Derbyshire ghost: the embodiment of all the men who have ever tried to tear a living from the rock. Not an individual; not even a phantom Brindley. He is the whole lot of them, lumped together: the Roman, the Saxon, the Dane – all the Peakrel lead-miners that ever there were. They believe in him very firmly in the village, quite like him, actually. He is said not to be malevolent. Not in the least. Unless you are up to something in one of his old workings that you shouldn't be.'

Kingsey suddenly swung round and barked at the servants.

'Parade dismissed! You have your work to do, and I can't have any more of your time wasted like this. It must be sadly obvious to Sergeant Brunt by now that none of us is able to help him.'

Brunt let it happen. There would be other ways of following such leads as he had picked up here, and in Kingsey's presence he was going to pick up no more. But even an attempt to side-track him was informative. Kingsey himself escorted him down to the entrance-hall.

'So. One presumes that a team of stallions would not keep the diligent sleuth away from Brindley's Quarter?'

'I'd certainly like to cast my eye over the spot.'

'You are welcome to wander anywhere you want about the estate. I wonder why Brindley's Quarter attracted this evidently introspective lass. Always on the look-out for a cache, do you think? Beyond the kitchen-yard you'll see the stables and beyond them a hillside that looks like the discarded butt-end of Creation. The litter is Brindley's.'

He actually, over-playing the image of geniality, put out a hand for Brunt to grip.

'Mind the Old Man doesn't get you, Sergeant.'

Chapter Seven

Brunt was content to go where Kingsey wanted him to. It was enough for the moment to know that Kingsey wanted to be able to account for his movements. He crossed the kitchen-yard and went round the back of the stables. Brindley's Quarter was not difficult to find – Brindley had certainly made an enduring mess of the hill-side. Even before the advent of Brindley, the prospect must have been frighteningly sterile, a reminder to passing man of his tenuous grip upon his planet. As Kingsey had said – the butt-end of Creation.

But Brindley had evidently not been a man to give in easily. It was doubtful whether he had ever got more out of his rake-end than enough to fill his Dish – the standard measure fixed by the Barmote Court to establish a miner's right. Brunt knew more about the ancient practices than he had cared to reveal to Kingsey. He found now a good deal of evidence of Brindley's activities: the foundations and an end-wall of Brindley's *coe*: his rough stone storeshed. The rotten framework of an old wooden sledge, used for dragging waste out of the working: Brindley's *corfe*. The rusted iron hoop from an old bucket: Brindley's *kibble*. Brunt scrambled up the tip-heap – Brindley's *deads* – and found himself in sight of the oblong slit in the rock face that had been Brindley's barren mine.

Brindley had obviously followed down a narrow fissure and driven his first boring along the line of a natural fault that made easier work for his pick. The gashes could still be seen where the pick head had slipped against the stone: scars a couple of centuries old. Brunt lowered his shoulders, the rock ceiling was nowhere more than five feet high, and walked some way into the working. His boots slopped through a stagnant puddle, the walls lined with a dank lichen. Then the floor became drier, though there was a stench from the droppings of the generations of bats that had housed there since Brindley's day. Daylight receded behind him, was blocked out by the breadth of his own shoulders. Brunt struck a match; it was immediately extinguished by a draught. He struck another and cupped it in his hand. It shone unnaturally yellow. Somewhere ahead of him water dripped in two separate places, an unpredictable cross-rhythm that could easily fray the nerves of a lonely man. Somewhere in a distant gallery a pebble fell: the Old Man? Still walking his galleries in search of an outcrop of the rake? There was small wonder that imaginations were active locally. Brunt turned and began to shuffle back towards the daylight. Outside, as he came up out of the fissure, the air was unbelievably warm and clean.

So why had Amy Harrington taken to coming here? Just to escape from the mockery of the servants' table? Didn't they breed them any tougher than that in Tapton these days? Hadn't a year in old Eleanor Copley's chimney-corner hardened her off? *Didn't know how to go on in a big house?* She had been three years at Rowsley. The Alloways were mill-owners, they ran an establishment of substance.

Was she stealing from Kingsey, and using the mine as a cache? Or had someone else got a cache there – someone from the Hall who was hoodwinking Kingsey? Had Amy Harrington been stupid enough to get herself mixed up in something? Had she merely suspected some mal-practice? Had she conceived some romantic notion, culled from her silly reading, of herself helping to bring the thief to book?

Brunt sauntered along the flattened summit of Brindley's *deads*. A narrow footpath skirted a weathered concavity in the rock-face and he found himself on a level grassy patch from which he could overlook the Hall. Someone had harnessed a governess' cart and he saw it set out along the estate road that was Kingsey's private link with the Staffordshire side.

There was a rabbit-warren up here. A part-grown animal was cleaning its whiskers heedless of Brunt's presence. Brunt began to search the terrain systematically, presently came upon a rabbit trap, one of a pattern with which he had become familiar on the hills between Matlock and the coal-field. A wooden peg some nine inches long was driven firmly into the ground, holding one end of a wire noose that was also joined to one arm of a powerful lateral spring. When an animal was up to its shoulders in the noose, the spring was released. Its upper arm shot up to the perpendicular, so that the rabbit was snatched off its feet and hung with its neck broken, its front paws hanging pathetically down, like those of a begging poodle.

What was curious was that there was actually a rabbit in this trap – a rabbit that had been in it for a very long time. Its fur had been soaked by dews and storms and dried in the Pennine winds – time and again. Its eye-sockets were empty and the head twisted and misshapen. A little way away he found a second trap. This one had caught a cat, a creature that had died with its upper lip curled savagely away from its teeth.

A third trap had caught a hen, a stray from someone's yard. To judge by the litter of feathers, the fowl had not given in easily. But a fox had partially liberated it, and Brunt found the feather-fan of a wing some distance away.

The bodies were all some months old. A few months ago some poacher had set his traps here for the last time. He could not have known then that he would not be coming back. He would not likely abandon his traps and catch.

Thos Beresford? Not unnaturally, the thought crossed Brunt's mind, and he dismissed it as a dangerously misleading impulse. There must be other poachers in Piper's Fold. Someone who had been warned off this particular warren? But wouldn't Thos and his friends have seen that as an irresistible challenge? And would not any gamekeeper sending them off have confiscated their gear?

It all pointed, Brunt felt sure, to the fact that someone had felt under a compulsion, for the last few months, to stay away from here. He continued to stave off his first wishful guess: there was no logic in jumping at Thos Beresford.

But then an intuitive certainty struck Brunt: Thos would know about it.

Chapter Eight

Brunt sat in the late afternoon in the musty, brown-walled inhospitality of his bedroom in the inn. Since his comparatively leisurely return from the lead working, nothing had happened. Piper's Fold was about its business, whatever that might be. A man mending a wall had been eager to touch his cap to him, and they had talked for a minute or two; about crows, for some reason.

Otherwise nothing. Brunt whiled away the time marshalling his notes so far; no useful new pattern emerged. Then someone knocked on his door, and after first trying to turn the knob the wrong way, Albert Potter came in.

A big man, a hairy man. Black, barely manageable hair in a spade beard that seemed forever to be wanting to get away at ill-considered angles; a man whose cheeks bore a discomforting resemblance to raw beef even when he was not, as at the moment, overheated from struggling up the Clough.

Detective-Constable Potter was an older man than Brunt, old enough to have been Brunt's mentor when Brunt was first transferred out of the uniformed wing. It was Potter who had taught Brunt how to be inconspicuous in a shop doorway; who had taught him to trail his quarry from the *opposite* side of the street. No one knew how old Potter really was. For a decade the rumour had been running round the stations that he was due for retirement next year; but he was still in the force. And if Piper's Clough had raised his blood-pressure, it was not because the gradient was too steep for him. It was because he would, naturally, have expected to cover the stretch at the same speed he would have walked a level, well-paved road. Potter was a great believer in steady progress.

Brunt was pleased to see him. He had not expected him until the next day. It was the first time that Potter had actually worked for him; but Potter was not the one to feel resentment at having to take orders from a former pupil. *I like to see the lads get on.* Brunt had heard him say it about others. Potter knew without being told why he himself would never be promoted.

'Did *you* come by train, Sergeant?'

No irony in the use of Brunt's rank. Brunt was a sergeant; that was it. Potter sat down like an inert load on the side of his sergeant's bed.

'Nearly,' Brunt said. 'I caught sight of its tail-lamps twice.'

'It's my first trip on the line. Our fastest stretch was sixteen miles three furlongs in four hours twelve minutes.' Potter was the living master of arcane detail. 'We stopped once while the train-crew went off for lunch at a pub. Our hopes were raised when the fireman came back after three-quarters of an hour. Big chap with a gigantic head ...'

'Jack Plant.'

'What he'd really come for was the driver's concertina. He went off across the fields with it, and they were gone another hour.'

'Anyway, you've been to Rowsley?'

'I have.'

Potter brought a sheaf of papers from his Gladstone bag. Paperwork was the bane and besetting failure of his life. He knew it, regretted it and yet was paradoxically proud of each creative sacrifice. Brunt read his report through once and was careful what he said next. One always had to be at least a little careful with Potter on the subject of literary composition. One would hesitate to point out to him, for example, that if one will begin one's preamble with *Whereas*, one must expect syntactical problems sooner or later. One had to remember that Potter was no mean policeman. In perception, Brunt rated him second to few – and in enthusiasm he was a giant apart.

'So: you went to Rowsley. And you formed the impression that the girl was *clean, sober, punctual and diligent?*'

'That's right.'

Potter was always pleased when one read aloud from his *incunabula* without active disapproval.

'Anything else about her?'

'Bit silly, I'd say.'

'In what sense? Simple-minded? Unreliable? Skittish? Giggly?'

'She couldn't have been any of those things, could she?'

'I don't know. Couldn't she?'

'If she had, the Alloways wouldn't have taken her to their hearts the way they did.'

'They did, did they?'

'No doubt about that.'

'So in what sense was she silly?'

Potter ran his fingers through his beard.

'I call it silly, chucking up a good home, plenty of outings, well thought of by all the family, by stealing something that was no real use to her.'

'Now steady, Albert. Let's take this a point at a time. A good home ...'

'It certainly was. Plenty of money about, for one thing, and not their master. The Alloways have never been servants themselves, so they know how to treat a servant. The girl always had the same to eat as them – I mean, apart from artichokes and asparagus, and that sort of bloody rubbish, which she wouldn't have liked anyway.'

'And outings, you said?'

'Always going somewhere: Matlock Bath, the Winnats, Hathersage. From late spring to early autumn they lived out of doors. Lovely gardens, roses and Christ knows what. And hardly any fire-places.'

'Fire-places?'

Potter answered as bitterly as if he had spent half his own life on his knees with a housemaid's box and a black-leading brush.

'For five or six months of the year she'd only the morning-room to do. And they have a gas-geyser in the bathroom, so she hadn't to go humping hot water up three flights of stairs every time some bugger felt a bit soiled. And half their meals were picnics – with

Amy Harrington passing the plates round – and eating off them herself a couple of minutes later.'

'Maybe she wasn't the sort to count her blessings.'

'Oh, but she was.' Potter looked positively hurt that he should be called on to substantiate the point.

'She was a nice girl, Sergeant. At home and at Sunday School she'd been taught to know her place. She used to sidle up to Mrs Alloway sometimes and tell her how grateful she was. Not smarmy, like; genuine. And Mrs Alloway loved the girl almost as if she were her own. That's what makes it so surprising . . .'

Brunt interrupted on a different note.

'Any men about?'

'Mr Alloway.' Potter shook his head emphatically.

'Nothing there – not what you're thinking. There was a son, a couple of years younger than Amy, only there in the school holidays. I tried to probe that, but it wasn't easy. Mrs Alloway's mind doesn't run along those channels at all. It wouldn't, would it, talking to me? But I'm pretty sure there wasn't anything there. Also there was a daughter, younger still. Amy used to do her sums for her, sometimes, behind the governess's back – and didn't always get them right. You see, Tom,' Potter really was surrendering to his enthusiasm now. 'There's no rhyme or reason about what Amy did.'

'What *did* she do?'

Potter rubbed a pliable nose with his knuckles. 'This is the curious thing. Mrs Alloway had missed a pair of Zylonite hair-brushes and a dressing-comb from her toilet-table.'

'What's Zylonite?'

'I don't know. That's what Mrs Alloway called it. These things were not specially valuable,' but they ought not to have gone astray. She searched high and low for them. Then she found Amy Harrington's bedroom door ajar. The girl had a woven split-cane hold-all, in which she'd brought her things over from Eleanor Copley's, and a corner of it was sticking out from under her bed, as if it had been recently moved. She opened it, and there were the missing articles. Of course, she beat the big drum about it. Told the girl she would have to go, and she was having the police in, and she'd have to write and tell her father. The silly thing is that she had no intention of doing anything of the sort. She was terribly upset by it. She couldn't for the life of her understand what had got into the girl – it was so completely out of character. But she saw no harm in scaring the wits out of her – giving the girl a rotten night in which to think things out. The next thing she knew, the girl had gone – split-cane hold-all and all.'

'Did she get in touch with the police?'

'She had the Rowsley sergeant over, and he said he'd set up a hue and cry if she wanted to bring charges, which she solidly refused to do.'

'She didn't write to the father?'

'She tortured herself about that. Started a letter and screwed it up several times. Amy had told her enough about what things were like at home for her to know that Harrington would have half killed the girl if he could have got hold of her.'

'He would, too. I once had a similar case.'

'The next thing, Mrs Alloway had a letter from the girl, announcing that she'd got this other job, apologising for all the worry she had caused, pleading not to have her future torn apart for her.'

'Admitting the theft?'

'Not in so many words. Mystifying. But fact is fact.'

'Any strangers in the house or district? You went into that?'

'Tried to. But it was eighteen months ago. You know what it's like trying to jog people's memory after a week.'

Brunt looked at his watch.

'*Find her*. That's my brief. I'm beginning to have an uneasy feeling about what state she'll be in. Time for a drink, Albert. Come downstairs, and with a bit of luck you'll hear a little inside information about the running of the old Cromford and High Peak. And thank you for your efforts in Rowsley. *Clean, sober, punctual and diligent*. A good report, Albert.'

'Thank you, Sergeant.'

They had been friends before, but it was cemented now.

Chapter Nine

'Of course, there are people who think that the Cromford and High Peak is run for the benefit of the general public, but those who've made a study of the matter know that it's really run for Thos Beresford's.'

Sammy Nall; the cadaverous, hungry story-teller who looked as if the feast he really craved for was a bottomless tale of universal calamity. Brunt had been looking forward to Potter's reactions to the Beresford legend, but somehow, now it was all starting up again, the prospect seemed less funny.

'Like that time he nearly ran out of coal on the way up to Bunsall. Thos liked to drop a lump or two off at Haslin Cottages, but this morning he'd missed them, either because he was short, or because it had got out of his head. Then, over by Belfield's Brow, he liked to make one of his stops. He always reckons to set his traps on the evening run, then look at them again on the morning round. And while he was off the engine, Jack Plant had to go up to Logan's farm for some eggs. When they came back, they found that someone from Haslin's had been and helped himself from the tender. Only whoever it was had overdone it. Thos reckoned he had enough left to get them up to Bunsall, but not enough for the return run. There was nothing for it but to reverse the train back to Haslin and try to get some of it back. Thos did that, right enough, but not before he'd got into a fight about it. Then his reversing gear stuck, and he had to half take it down and put it together again. And while they were doing that, they let the old engine get off the boil, so they had to scrape the clinker out and make a fresh start on the fire. Then Thos spilled his tea, because he had a loose regulator valve that kept falling shut, and he'd had to hang his can over the handle to keep it open. So they had to stop at Tommy Ashmore's place to brew a fresh lot. And ten or twenty passengers waiting up at Bunsall with a wind lashing down from the *Cat and Fiddle* that had their clothes flapping round them like the sails of a China clipper.'

'Thos is supping a lot of ale these days,' somebody said.

'Yes, and if some of these gentry who've come up to see the hills could see the state he was in at the throttle, they'd get out and walk. The way he hangs on to that handle nowadays, there's no danger of it falling shut. Mind you, he says that old engine doesn't need to be driven: it knows its own way round. One afternoon he nearly forgot to stop at Dowlow Halt, but the old engine knew. He says he felt the brakes go on of their own accord.'

'It could have been Jack Plant, of course.'

'Jack knows how to keep him on the rails without upsetting him.'

Then a newcomer came in, a wiry but rugged, elderly little man, whom nobody referred to by any name but Blucher – pronunciation strictly anglicised.

'Old Nought-Four-Nought not in yet?'

'Give him another half hour. A man with two wives has to spend some time at home.'

'When Thos strikes the road tonight, it'll happen be with but one intent.'

'How's that, then, Blucher?'

'The Rector's had old Juggler dig old Thos's patch.'

Old Juggler was the sexton, a man who stood in a peculiar relationship to the habitués of *The Crooked Rake*. Fundamentally he was one of them, and in a general way he was given special dispensation because of his unavoidable closeness to authority; but they only half forgave him for it, and did not trust him.

'He can't do that,' someone said. 'Old Thos always says he can't be touched as long as he has a crop in the ground.'

'His crop's out of the ground. Old Juggler had to sack his taters and wheel them round to Thos's on a barrow.'

Some man smacked his lips over his ale. Any crowd enjoys seeing a pebble slung at a giant.

'So which of Thos's missuses was in when Juggler called?'

'Both on 'em,' Blucher said.

'And which one answered the door?'

'Both on 'em.'

A renewed silence had a tinge of respect in it.

'And is Juggler still in one piece?'

A man with the lining sticking out of the side of his cap went up to have his pot refilled.

'So what'll Thos do now, do you reckon?'

'Have that fire he's always promised us, up at the Stump.'

'He's been talking for weeks of burning an effigy of the Captain. Happen he'll chuck the Rector on the same pile.'

'Fat lot of bloody good that will do.'

'It worked years ago. The Rector climbed down about the gravediggers' ale.'

'He was only a young man in those days, not so sure of his ground.'

Brunt risked a direct intervention. 'What does he want to burn an effigy of the Captain for?'

But this was too much for them. Brunt knew he had made a mistake. They looked uneasily at each other, no one prepared to answer. At last someone felt obliged to come to Beresford's defence.

'You don't have to take too much notice of everything Thos says.'

Brunt was aware that he was observing a watershed in the affairs of the *Rake*. Yesterday Thos had been the undisputed tribal champion. Now the sling had been wielded. Was he going to scratch his temple in casual annoyance? Or was this going to prove a mortal blow? Clearly there were men here who thought it was; but they lacked the confidence to say so yet.

Supper was brought for the two policemen, but not by the girl from Bristol. It was served by the landlord's wife, a nonentity of whom little was seen about the inn, who rarely spoke and even less often smiled. The food was the same as yesterday: cold meat, pickles and cheese – and what had yesterday seemed highly gratifying was now beginning to look a little sorry for itself.

They had almost finished their meal when they heard hooves in the yard. But this time Thos did not address his horse with any jocular remarks. He even seemed to have lost the knack of the years, for the front door jammed in front of him, and he had to lunge savagely at it with his shoulder. He passed through the length of the bar without looking at anyone. His tankard was taken from its hook on a rafter and filled for him. Jack Plant followed him and closed the door with the confident gentleness of a big man.

Beresford took back his first pint in a draught, then asked for another. When it had been drawn, he brought it across and set it down aggressively on the table amidst Brunt's and Potter's plates. Then, without waiting for an invitation, he slid his body over the bench opposite them.

'You two gentlemen can help me. I want you to go and arrest the Rector.'

His eye-brows were working furiously, alternating between wild interrogation and murderous menace.

'That,' Brunt said, 'might not be your neatest course to satisfaction. He would almost certainly be discharged within minutes. Any bench of justices would be sure to stop the hearing. In which case you would lose considerable face, and I would probably have to come prospecting for lead for a living.'

'Is that so?'

'That is so,' Brunt said soberly, and Potter nodded.

The eye-brows looked as if they themselves would be prepared to take on the Rector single-handed. And Brunt understood in that moment that it was unfair to judge the man by those brows – or even to try to interpret them. He was their victim, rather than their master. He was in similar case to one of his wives – the little tubby one, who appeared to smile.

'In that case, I must ask you gentlemen for the benefit of your superior education.'

'A debatable premise,' Brunt said. 'But we'll do our best.'

'Is it or is it not the law of this land that a man cannot be evicted from a plot on which he has a growing crop?'

'Again, debatable – and it does not fall within our province. It is a point of civil law – one on which I think the lawyers would grow fat whilst you went thin. I'm sorry, Thos, but I'm afraid you'll have to ask your solicitor.'

'You mean you're too bloody scared.'

'Too bloody scared,' Brunt agreed amicably. 'I always am bloody scared when the law can't make its own mind up.'

The eye-brows remained in penetrating immobility for some seconds. But the remark seemed to appeal to Beresford's streak of reason; it was honestly self-effacing, and this may have convinced him that it was therefore sound. He slewed round, thumped the table and addressed the whole company.

'In that case, we shall have to burn the bugger. There's nowt else for it. Next Tuesday. We'll have the biggest bloody fire since the Relief of Inkerman.'

No one repeated their doubts. After a brief pause, Blucher summed up the feeling of the meeting.

'Aye. We'll have a bloody fire, then.'

There were murmurs of agreement, but no great enthusiasm. Brunt turned to Beresford. It was time to get him on to something else.

'I'm sorry we can't be much help to you, Thos. Because you could be of considerable help to us.'

'Always willing to try, providing it'll cost me nowt.'

'We've been wondering who's not been attending to his traps.'

'What traps?'

'On Brindley's Quarter.'

'I expect somebody hasn't had time to get round,' Beresford said, unpersuasively.

'Somebody hasn't had time to get round for six months or so, judging by the state of the carcases.'

And at this Beresford seemed to become unaccountably angry, though it showed itself only in the area of white of eye that became visible. Brunt sought for possible explanations. It was hardly likely, in the final count, that these traps were Thos's own. The man could not have time, in the midst of all his other activities, to be the only poacher in the village. But perhaps he delegated strips of likely territory to other men. Divide and rule: it was a well tried principle.

Beresford lifted himself back over the bench and stood with his palms on the table, both arms straight.

'Have you said anything about this to anybody else, Sergeant?'
'No.'
'Then don't – for twenty-four hours. Leave it to me.'
'Done, Thos, for twenty-four hours.'

Beresford left them and walked slowly back to the counter, where he leaned outwards to face the circle.

'No bugger's asked me yet what my rappit's been up to today.'
'Aye, let's have a rappit story, Thos.'

Détente. They were back to nearly normal. But Brunt had the feeling that it was probably going to be shortlived. He beckoned curtly to Potter and they left the bar as if to go up to their rooms. But by the foot of the stairs, by the door which led into the kitchen, Brunt stopped, put in his head and called to the landlord's wife.

'Is Mildred not about today, then?'
'You won't be seeing any more of Mildred.'
'No? Has she taken against us, then?'
'I've taken against her.'

She was clattering dishes in the sink, making it clear that her work meant more to her than any conversation with the law.

'Sorry to hear that,' Brunt said.
'Yes, well, it's been coming on for some time.'

She turned and brought a pile of plates to the dresser.

Brunt had to step sideways out of her way.

'So you've given her her money, have you?'
'She's away on the Fly in the morning. Till then she's in her room.'
'There are some questions that I want to ask her.'

The landlady shrugged her shoulders. 'Go and try, if you want to. If she'll open her door for you.'

She went to another cupboard. Brunt had to move again. She seemed determined to turn him into an obstacle.

'And these questions that you've got on your mind. They have nothing to do with this house or the way it is conducted. You might as well understand that for a start.'

'Is that why you've given her the bullet?'

'She's had it coming to her for some time.'

But would it have happened if Brunt had never turned up here? In the bar, they could hear Beresford reaching tonight's climax.

'They've both been on to me about this bloody mangle, and it's got so I had to do it before I left the house this morning. Ball bearings all over the bloody yard, and you can be certain I had to lose one. It rolled off somewhere under a pile of tackle. But I saw th'owd rappit lifting its latch, and it's straight down there under a stack of old plant-pots, brings me this ball-bearing back in its teeth. Its eyesight is better than mine, you see. That was the time, it killed a ferret . . .'

But they did not linger to hear that one out. Brunt led the way up the stairs. He had not bothered to ask which was Mildred's bedroom. He went straight up to the attics, and there were two doors opening off a dingy landing. One stood open to reveal a cluttered boxroom. Brunt tapped on the other.

There was no reply. Through a soot-streaked lattice window at the other end of the passage they could see the hills about the Hall, the crest of the rise that enfolded Brindley's Quarter. Brunt rapped again. Still no answer. He nodded to Potter that he had thought of a dodge. He stooped with his lips close to the key-hole and began to sing – not especially musically –

> *So it's away, boys, away,*
> *To Californ-i-a,*
> *There's plenty of gold, so I've been told,*
> *On the banks of Sacramento.*

Melodramatic; shades of Blondin; but it might just catch her imagination. At first it looked as if the appeal was going to fail.

And then they heard her come across the room, the rattle of a bolt. The door opened and she stood there in her night-clothes, thick, dark hair loose about her shoulders; dark, but with a touch of deep redness somewhere in it, almost as if she had a streak of Irish in her. Perhaps she had.

'Two of you! I should be proud of myself.'

No sign of fear; resigned defiance. The resemblance to some wench from a dock-side tavern was stronger than ever – and not just a readiness to join in the lewd singing. She was hardened. She thought she knew every wile that could be used against her. But she was not very far from the end of her tether, either. She could be provoked perhaps a little further.

Well-rounded breasts unsupported under the loose fabric of her night-gown. High colour in her cheeks; a tiny black mole at the side of her neck. Her eyes flashed bitterness at Brunt; she was affecting to ignore Potter. Brunt thought he knew the drill for the likes of her. Her defiance was not yet at its peak. She had to be pushed over that top. Then something would burst. She had to collapse first, then you could start building.

'So you think you'll do a better business in the big city?'

'I'm not here to do business with you, if that's what you're playing for.'

'Chance would be a fine thing.'

'Clever devil, aren't you? I'm leaving here because I want to leave here.'

'Oh, yes?'

Brunt stepped right into the room, ushered Potter in as well and closed the door behind them. Mildred's hold-all, a box of woven cane, exactly like the one of Amy Harrington's that they had talked about – almost the badge of office for a female servant on the move – was standing on a chair ready packed, the lid not yet in place. Brunt picked it up and emptied its contents on to the bed, picking up odd articles of clothing and shaking out their folds. It was a pretty miserable collection, threadbare as much from washing as from wearing: two pairs of long-cloth drawers, a plain chemise, yellowing with age.

'When you've done!' she said.

'Just looking for the ancestral plate.'

'Listen, policeman, the day you find me lifting someone else's property . . .'

'Like at Gloucester? Or did they run you out for soliciting?'

'Soliciting? Sergeant Brunt, there are some things I've never done.'

'Not even for Captain Kingsey?'

'I never did,' she said, and the tears were starting out of her eyes at last, but not convulsive flowing ones. This was the dry, burning rage, passionate resentment of injustice.

'Why do you think I came away from there? At the Hall I didn't, and here I haven't, and at Gloucester and Bristol I didn't. Why do you think I left home in the first place? I've seen too much of it, I tell you. I'll go with a man one day, but he'll be mine, and I'll do the picking.'

Brunt let the immediate wave spend itself and began to refold some of her garments, not deftly, but showing a will.

'You can leave those alone. They'll all have to be washed again now you've had your dirty maulers on them.'

'So who's going to see them tomorrow night, when you've got to town? All right, save it, Mildred. You've held out till now – maybe. So how much longer? How far do you think you're going to get tomorrow?'

She looked at him with absolute hatred, her lips tight: she had undoubtedly asked herself the same question.

'So why are they getting rid of you, Mildred? Because of something that Kingsey might do to you as he did to Amy Harrington? Or are you afraid of what might happen to you here in *The Crooked Rake?*'

'Because I'm trouble, that's why. Because *you're* here. Because *you* can't leave well alone.'

'Oh, aye? Well, I ask you again: how far do you think you're going to get tomorrow?'

'I've got my fare to Derby,' she said sulkily. 'Nadin's given me that.'

'Derby? Oh, aye? Well, you'll find some nice big furnace-man to fancy you in Derby, perhaps – chap with China clay all dried out down the front of his vest.'

She picked up a pair of woollen combinations from the bed and began beating him about the head and shoulders with them. And then, when Potter started chuckling, she turned on him and began to belabour him too. He pulled the garment out of his straggling black beard and took a step towards her as if he were going to pinion her arms to her sides. There were limits to Potter's patience.

'Leave her to me, Albert.'

The girl cowered away from them, unable to believe that Brunt would not now set about her. He went on talking quietly.

'So it's to be Derby next? And I've no doubt that you've got a few odd shillings saved up. I know your type: careful. But how much longer do you think you can go on just managing to win? You might be able to keep yourself for a week, perhaps two, then what? If you don't get a job – and there's taverns and dining-rooms in Derby where they might not ask too many questions – but I reckon that those are the very ones you'll want to keep away from. You've held out till now, you say. Suppose I believe you? How much longer do you think you're going to make it? Mildred – you'd better let me give you an address in Derby that you can go to.'

'Oh, yes? I think I know where that might be.'

The Bristol brogue was very strong now; but she was a tough specimen.

'It's what you might call plain cooking, isn't it – bread, water and gruel?'

'Put it another way, then. I'll give you a few addresses that you'd do as well to stay away from. Mildred, you'll have me thinking that there really was something in Gloucester for which they've still got a warrant out. I don't know anything about that and I'd lean over backwards not to find out, if I thought it might help me with my bigger fish. And you know who my big fish is, don't you?'

She was more placid now, in control of herself, but still not prepared to commit herself to the narrow chance that he might be talking in good faith.

'All right, Mildred. I don't blame you. A girl wants to keep herself to herself, doesn't she? Some girls, anyway. For as long as they can. But think about it, lass, if you happen to sleep badly tonight. Think about it some more. I'll still be about in the morning when you get up. Go on thinking about it on the train; it isn't exactly a hurried journey. Think about it when you get to Derby. And any time until that last moment when the system's beaten you, drop in at any police station and say that the man you want to talk to is called Brunt.'

He opened the door with one hand behind his back and signalled to Potter. Potter thought at first that he wanted to be left alone with the girl; but Brunt was out on the landing on his heels.

'Give her time, Albert. That's something that we haven't quite run out of yet. There are odd moments when I can't help feeling in a general way that there might be a touch of honesty about that lass.'

Brunt went to his room whistling *The Banks of Sacramento*.

Chapter Ten

Brunt was up and about early the next morning: a morning of crisp, chilly sunshine, autumn flexing its fingers, but not yet having taken its grip. It was going to be one of those exhilarating days, summer clearly over, but yellow weeds still flowering, the straggling dead grasses still rustling in dried out gullies. From a vantage point high on the flank of Piper's Clough he watched Thos Beresford ride old Nought-Four-Nought down to the railway track: a burly, forceful figure of a man, occasionally kicking the horse's flanks with impatient heels. Brunt had wondered how a man on horse-back negotiated the difficult valley bottom. Beresford was not relying on the dried out stream bed at all. He followed a ridge-track up on the western slope. Only when he came in sight of the C. and H.P. Halt did he actually ease his horse down from the hill. And no magic or great skill of field-craft was needed for Brunt to keep the man under observation from his ambush: all he had to do was arrive there first; the natural features did the rest. Brunt was sure that Beresford had not seen him.

After he had watched the engine driver off to work, Brunt climbed back into the village. Here he called on Mrs Hallum, the deaf old woman who had handed him her five-piastre piece. She too, it seemed, was an early riser and was busy at odd jobs in and out of her house. She seemed genuinely glad to see him, immediately ready to co-operate in the plan that he suggested.

Brunt returned to *The Crooked Rake*, enjoying an almost schoolboy satisfaction at having his breakfast served to him while Potter was still abed. And yet Potter was not the man ever to be five minutes behind on a trick. Perhaps it was the strong air of the hill-country that was making him unusually tired. Brunt did not wait his meal for him; and halfway through it, Potter came briskly in – from outside. He must have been abroad even earlier than Brunt – and Brunt had not set eyes on him in the village.

'Ah, Albert, you'll be going back on this morning's Fly. The train's due at the Halt at about ten. The only thing we can be certain of is that it won't leave before time.'

Potter's face fell – there was no doubting the aptness of the cliché. His eyes no longer wanted to meet Brunt's, the corners of his mouth lost their spirit. But Potter was too deeply schooled in the discipline of the force – or, at least, a large part of him was – to offer any argument against a sergeant, even against a new one whom he had had a hand in training.

Nothing official had been said to Brunt about his retaining Potter as his assistant. If there were a dire emergency here in Piper's Fold, this could doubtless be arranged – given time, patience and propitious communications – or convenient lack of them. But Potter had only come here with a message. Brunt had no prescriptive right to hold on to him.

'There are things I want you to do for me, Albert. In this order, please – and let me have the answers and confirmation as quickly as you can.'

Potter brought out a slip of paper from his pocket-book and got ready to take notes beside his breakfast plate.

'First, put the Superintendent abreast about how things stand up here. I don't think I've been up to anything I shouldn't – so far – so it'll do if you put it down in your own words.'

'In writing?' Potter asked, with a touch of stoicism.

'Try and get away with a verbal report if you can. Then I want you to go digging round the foundations of the Isaac Mosley case. I don't mean just the fencing that he's gone to prison for. If there'd been anything other than the Turkish relics that touched on Piper's Fold, I expect it would have been in my brief. But have a look at anything that still looks a shade doubtful – cases uncleared, works of art that might have vanished into the unknown, and might have got there with a helping hand from Isaac Mosley. I've often wondered what sort of mentality it is that gets a kick out of possessing treasures that he daren't show to another living soul. I dare say Kingsey might prove quite informative on that score. And take a description of his man Fletcher – the one with the sleek hair and side-boards. Kingsey describes him as his steward. He's probably given a good deal of latitude in buying pictures, and maybe takes his own rake-off on the side.'

Potter made notes unemotionally. The inn was extraordinarily quiet this morning. The landlord's wife had brought their food and dutifully returned their goodmornings, but said no more. Nadin himself was not to be seen; there was no sign of life from Mildred.

'Then, if you can find the time – well, make the time, it won't be wasted – I want to know if there's anything on paper anywhere about Thos Beresford's marital status. I've got the feeling at the back of my mind that it might be useful to know.'

That was all. With pencil poised, Potter was waiting for more. Brunt had not asked him what he himself had been up to this morning. It occurred to him now that a matter of only a few weeks ago, if he had chanced to meet Potter in an office corridor, they would have stopped and gossiped about the cases that they both had on hand. And Brunt would not have hesitated to tap Potter for ideas. There was no consistent streak of brilliance, but he did have his bright moments. Brunt did his best to smile honestly across the breakfast table.

'Albert, it's no time at all since I'd have been asking you what you'd do next. I'm still in the market.'

Potter brought out his pocket-book again and sorted out a piece of paper covered with hieroglyphics.

'Plan of the rake,' he said briefly.

'What do you want a plan of the *Rake* for? Frightened you'll go walking into the wrong bedroom?'

'I don't mean this place. I mean the old main seam – the crooked rake itself. I was up at Brindley's Quarter at first light. On my way back I got talking to an old-timer at his cottage. He gave me an idea of how the seam ran, and I've had a shot at mapping it out.'

Brunt looked at the sketch. It suggested nothing to him.

'I've come to the conclusion,' Potter said, 'that Brindley was a little naughty.'

'And well he may have been. But Brindley lived in the seventeenth century. He's safe from the likes of us, Albert. How was he naughty?'

'I don't think he got any ore at all out of that working of his. Not even enough to fill his *dish*. That mine was *salted*, Sergeant; he showed the Barmote Court his gleanings, but he gathered them elsewhere.'

'That's been done before and since. There's not much point in it unless you can find some mug to buy a share in your holding. I'm sorry, Albert, but I don't see how it helps us. We've enough to worry about, without going back two hundred years.'

'But suppose that Brindley was up to something else, as well. Like, for instance, driving a *heading* into someone else's *grove*.'

Potter, as well as Brunt, was surprisingly informed about the customs and terminology of the Old Man.

'So what do you propose, Albert? A posthumous charge in front of the Barmaster?'

Potter showed calculatedly strained patience.

'If this were my case, I'd be wanting a good look inside that mine. Especially since the girl used to hang about there a lot.'

Of course, Potter was right. The fact was staring Brunt in the eyes, making him almost guilty of dereliction of duty over the last forty-eight hours.

'All right, Albert. You can stay here one more day. I'll take the responsibility.'

And was there the suspicion of a smile, playing somewhere beneath the black undergrowth of Potter's beard?

'Because any man who tackles a derelict mine single-handed is a fool. A couple doing it together are not much better. We shall need gear, Albert . . .'

'Lanterns, candles, balls of string . . .'

'What do we want balls of string for?'

'Sometimes several galleries run off at a cross-roads. You unwind string behind you to find your way back.'

'All right, Ariadne. You assemble what equipment you can. Do it without letting the village know what we are up to. I've got other work to do this morning, and time is creeping on.'

Brunt left the inn before there was any sign of movement from the Nadins or Mildred and passed through the village without allowing himself to be caught in conversation with anyone. After a little brief reconnaisance in the upper reaches of the Clough, he chose himself a spot not far down the track along which he had watched Beresford ride and took up a position behind a lichened pillar of rock, where he would be invisible to anyone coming down from the Fold.

For some twenty minutes he had the valley to himself. The sunshine was warmer now; a current of air played about the heavy corners of Brunt's eyes and made him realise how tired he felt. A jackdaw, wheeling about over a pile of rubble, protested at first at his presence, but became accustomed to him within minutes. Down in the bottom of the Clough, too far away for him to hear the rush of water in the swallows under the stones, two smaller birds quarrelled, squared up to each other in mid-flight, then disappeared behind a patch of scrub to continue their primeval battle over territorial rights.

Then Brunt saw the couple coming down from the village: Mildred in front, carrying her baggage under one arm, walking in uneven steps with her eyes glued to the rough ground. She was wearing an outdoor coat that Brunt had not seen before, brown with closely spaced buttons – not new, not well styled, but the girl's well husbanded best. Behind her, perhaps a yard and a half, walked Nadin, practised loping steps that seemed ungainly in his heavy boots, his arms swinging free, his hands empty. Brunt waited until they had drawn abreast of a gorse-bush that masked him obliquely from them. Then he stood up from his concealment and advanced to surprise them. The girl let out a little squeak and lurched sideways to prevent herself from falling.

'We're on our way down to the Halt,' Nadin said, as if assuring finality.

'There are one or two things I want to talk to her about. One or two things I've asked her to think over.'

'You'll have her miss her train,' Nadin said, coming down beside her, and trying to place himself protectively between the two of them – impossible because of the narrowness of the track.

'Doubtful,' Brunt said. 'I wouldn't put it past Thos Beresford to wait, knowing in advance that he's got a passenger. In any case, I'm offering her her last chance not to need that train.'

'You've no call to be delaying us,' Nadin said.

'I'm not delaying you. I'm delaying her. You've no standing in her life – except as a bully, and somebody else's toady.'

Nadin looked at Brunt as if the only next thing he knew was to come to blows. But Brunt, stocky, grotesque, ugly, was to any man's eyes the younger and fitter man. He took a step sideways and upwards so that he was looking down at the inn-keeper; and Nadin was on the outer side of the path, the ground falling away steeply below him.

'Your writ doesn't run to this sort of caper, Brunt.'

'My writ runs wherever its little legs will carry it.'

Meanwhile, the girl was looking at Brunt expectantly, puzzled, but showing no signs of fear; and astoundingly attractive, in spite of her misery. A man must be made of rock, not to be drawn to her by her sheer physical ebullience.

'Go home!' Brunt said to Nadin, exaggerating his contempt like a bad actor. 'You've paid her off, haven't you?'

Nadin did not move. Brunt turned to Mildred.

'Sleepless night? So you've done a little thinking?'

'I don't know what to think,' the girl said, not meeting his eyes. Nadin spoke to her.

'You don't have to wonder where you'll end up if you let him do your thinking for you.'

'Go home!' Brunt said again. 'Just remember you're an innkeeper. And you rely for your living on the licensing justices. And I'm a policeman. And I'm coming back to spend a few more nights under your roof whether I'm on speaking terms with you and your wife or not. And you're turning over in your mind how you're going to get rid of me. Well, I'll tell you this: you can't. You're not used to the law up in Piper's Fold, are you? And if it's Kingsey you're afraid of, because you're harbouring a woman who's on the run from him, you'd better start asking yourself whether you wouldn't be safer in my hands. As the girl is going to be.'

Nadin could find no argument. For an instant it looked as if he were going to fall back on his stupidity and repeat everything he had already said. But he simply stood silent, exhausted of ideas.

'Go home. She has nothing more to do with you.'

True as it was, Nadin seemed psychologically incapable of tearing himself away from them. He stood looking at them, a useless man, his hands dangling, wanting to fight, but not daring to.

Brunt knew that something else was true, too – something that he had just said: the valley and the village were fundamentally lawless – nearly as lawless as in the day of the Turkish pedlar. They could be visited by magistrates, who would deal indignantly with any poacher or his like who might be brought before them. They fell under the purview of a constable, who roamed an archipelago of hamlets between Harpur Hill and Hollinsclough – and who knew to the last tittle how far he dared go, both with the Peakrels and with his own superiors. They could be descended on from time to time by the likes of Brunt. A man who worked alone and committed a major crime need not be confident of getting away with it, not now in 1875. But if the community as a whole chose to defend a secret, they could still take a chance on winning the day. Then it was the law that stood alone. And the law, for the moment, was represented by Brunt alone.

He let his eyes wander over the back-cloth, the far green, scarred flank of the valley, the limestone pillars twisted into uncouth shapes. He was standing alone against a tradition as stubborn and ignorant as the Old Man himself. He ought to have been afraid, yet he was not afraid at all. Was that because the sun was shining? Because he was going soft in his head? Was he being lulled into false confidence by the sheer stupidity of a man like Nadin? Was he forgetting that what it could not understand, the Clough could think only of destroying? Was Brunt's imagination short-changing him?

He held out his arms for the girl to hand him her hold-all. She passed it to him and he signed to her to start climbing back up the hill. Nadin still stood in their path.

'Go on!' Brunt said to the girl, who took one step, hesitated and looked back at him over her shoulder.

'Go on!'

At last Nadin stepped aside. They both walked past him. The landlord began to continue his way down the valley: intent, now, probably, on reporting events to Beresford when the Fly passed. And, freed from the sight of him, the girl began to scramble vigorously upwards. Brunt balanced her burden on his shoulder and followed.

'I've found a place in the village where you can stay for a few days. That will give us time to work a few things out. But you can come and go as you please. If you really fancy chancing your arm in Derby, that's up to you. You don't have to ask my permission, though I'll admit it would suit my book for you to stay here.'

They rounded a fold in the cleft. They would be in the village in another five minutes.

'The woman you'll be staying with is deaf. I hope you won't find her too trying. She has a good heart.'

Mildred did not answer. She did not turn her head. Brunt had no inkling whether she had heard a word that he had said. The sunlight brought out the red tinge in her thick, dark hair.

So who was going to pay the old woman for her keep? Brunt had every reason to fear that his department's auditors would jib at footing that kind of bill. In which case, he would simply have to fork out for himself; not the first time he had been reminded of the Good Samaritan in this valley. It went against the grain, to pay out for what ought to be the responsibility of public funds. But there had been policemen in the past, hundreds to come in the future, who would dip into their pockets to break a case.

The old woman was waiting for them at her cottage gate, took Mildred into her home as if she were a daughter of her own who had just returned on the Fly from years of profligacy in the city. She had agreed at once to Brunt's suggestion.

'Goodbye for now. I'll be back later in the day.'

Brunt was anxious to get to Potter, to see what ropes and lanterns he had assembled. The girl, he thought, would be ready now to talk, but he wanted readiness to develop into urgency. He believed that the urgency would be hastened by the frustration of talking to the old woman. And he wanted Mildred to be affected by the cool silence of the cottage. But she did not want to wait.

'Sergeant Brunt, you're going away? There are things I've got to tell you.'

'I'll be back presently.'

'No, now.'

Tears that she could not check began to run down her cheeks; not the burning drought of yesterday's resentment. The old woman was brewing tea from her meagre larder. Brunt drew up a rush-covered chair for himself at the table.

Chapter Eleven

'Perhaps you've never been to Bristol, Sergeant Brunt?'

'I've been in other places, perhaps some of them worse.'

Mildred shook her head with unassailable certainty.

'There's no place worse than Bristol. I can remember the miseries of Bristol when I was only three years old. I can remember it as clearly as a picture. I can remember sitting on the stairs because we could not get into our room. My mother had gone off somewhere, and for some reason or other she had taken the key. She did go off sometimes, and we never knew how long it was going to be for. My father, he went off for even longer spells. And in between, my mother brought new fathers for us home; at least, that's what she tried to tell us.'

Mildred laughed cynically.

'When I think of some of those men that she brought home, it makes me realise why we were always glad to see our own father back. I remember sitting on those stairs. I couldn't tell you where in Bristol the building was, but I can still see those stairs. There's a certain smell, I don't know what it is. You don't get it in Piper's Fold. But if I were to smell it again, like I did once in Derby, when we were on our way here, I'd think I was back on those stairs.'

Rotting woodwork and fly-blown remnants of old food, damp plaster, leaking sewage; she wouldn't be smelling it here, in this cottage kitchen. The little house smelled of bread and ironing, drying herbs and a curl of blue wood-smoke escaping from the grate.

'I suppose we were hungry, and we must have been tired, but most of all I know that we were scared – yet I was too young to know about being scared. I was scared because I knew the others were. I've often tried to work out how many of us there were on those stairs that night, but I've never been absolutely certain. I know that I must have been the youngest bar two. And there was one little bit of heaven that we were cottoning on to, cottoning on to it because it was a sudden idea that had gone from mouth to mouth: the Poor House. We'd been frightened silly of the Poor House all our lives: my mother used to threaten us with it, when she was desperate to get her way about something. Now, suddenly, the Poor House was warm and dry, and they'd give us something to eat and drink. My brother Michael – he'd be nine or ten and he wasn't even supposed to be in charge of us – my sister Aileen was in charge of us, but Michael had a way, sometimes, of making all the others listen to him. He said he was going round to the Poor House to ask them to take us in. But then he came back and it was no good, they wouldn't have us. He'd even been to see Mr Stevenson, and I don't know now who Mr Stevenson was, but it had been brave of Michael to go and knock on his door. And Mr Stevenson went round with Michael to the Poor House, but they wouldn't take us in, not even for him. I don't know how it all ended up. I must have fallen asleep. I can't remember now where I woke up, but somehow things must have got better before they got worse again.'

The old woman had made a pot of tea and was sitting in her own chair, rocking it gently. It was doubtful how much she could follow of what was being said, but her eyes were fixed solemnly on Mildred's face. Perhaps there was something more expressive than words that she could understand.

'You don't know how bad Bristol is, Sergeant Brunt. These people here in Piper's Fold – they think they're rough. They're proud of themselves whenever they can kid each other that they're breaking the law. They don't know what breaking the law is. They make me laugh. I could tell you stories about Bristol: I could tell you about an old man of seventy-two who got six months' hard labour for interfering with his own grandchild, only eight. And he'd had her by his own daughter.'

Brunt could have capped the story, but he held his tongue. There was a certain charm, still, about her anger. She was a girl of passionate standards. Whence had she derived them, and how had she managed to maintain them? He was not going to risk impeding the flow by any interruption.

'My sister Aileen went off on the night train to London when she was thirteen. There were stories about the wealth and magic that that train could whisk you off to, and nobody believed them, not even those that went. But Aileen, of course, didn't go of her own accord. She went because money changed hands all along the line, and there was even a pound or two of it left over for my mother before the line ran out. There was good money – and I reckon there still is – for any country girl in London who was still fresh. You know what I mean? There weren't all that many of them still fresh by the time they were thirteen. But there were ways and means of passing yourself off as a beginner, even if you weren't – and not too difficult if the man happened to be drunk, as he usually was. And you won't perhaps believe this, Sergeant Brunt – it wasn't men who were running the traffic – not, at any rate, from the Bristol end. It was women. Two of them, Mrs Elliot and Miss Carpenter, looking for all the world as if they'd strayed out of a missionary lecture. They had a compartment twice a month on the night train for London out of Bristol, looking as if they were taking their little band of cherubs to a Charity School.'

On the wall of the cottage was a framed print of a picture called *The Squire's Call*: a hygenically scrubbed and immaculately dressed young villager's wife, cutting a slice of cake at the table for a benevolent old patriarch, sitting ram-rod straight in the only armchair.

'When Aileen went, I knew that my own turn would come – even though my mother would sometimes tell me, those times that she felt like talking to me, that she hoped things would change, and I wouldn't have to go. Things change, Sergeant Brunt? Things never will change, will they, unless you set yourself to try to make them change? But I mustn't ramble. The night train. I got so that I was looking forward to it, because I knew what I was going to do, and I thought it was going to be so simple. Go to London with Mrs Elliot and Miss Carpenter? There were men in London who'd pay twenty pounds in notes – most of it to Mrs Elliot and Miss Carpenter – to spend a night with a girl who hadn't been with a man before. Very fine; and once a girl had been with a man, what then? That was when I decided I was going to choose my own man, in my own time. I'd seen enough of the men that my mother had brought home. I suppose I always have been a rebel. There may have been times when I haven't done myself the best turn that I might have done. But there's one thing that I've had my own way about till now.'

Brunt thought he was beginning to understand the nature of her pride and determination. It wasn't something that anyone had taught her. It wasn't virtue, in the moralising sense. It was something more like sheer bloody obstinacy.

'Of course, I had several plans up my sleeve about how I was going to give them the slip off that train.' Mildred laughed.

'My God, when I think of how little I knew! London was just somewhere for me that lay at the other end of the earth. I couldn't have told you the names of three big towns that we'd pass on the way. If things had been left to the way I'd planned them, I wouldn't have ended up far from the end of the track myself. It didn't even occur to me that those two bitches, the missionaries – I still think of them as missionaries – would be on the look-out for one of us to try to escape. I must have thought of myself as the most original minded kid of twelve in the country. However, escape I did – but only because I was lucky. There was no planning about it, the way it worked out in the end. We stopped somewhere. There were oil-lamps and porters' barrows, and steam coming up from somewhere under the running-boards, and we were going to be there twenty minutes while they coupled another engine on. And Mrs Elliot and Miss Carpenter trooped us out – there were four of us on this trip – so that we could go to the lavatory while they stood guard at the door. I was beginning to be scared, to tell you the truth. I'd been looking for chances all night, but there hadn't been any. I'd even got to the state of thinking of opening the carriage door and hurling myself out beside the track. Not that I would have done, but my mind was spinning round like mad. Then suddenly, on that station, Gloucester it was, I found that I'd got parted from the others. I've no idea to this day how it happened. It can only have been for a split second, but by God I moved fast. There was a lot of noise, and people coming and going all over the place. Mrs Elliot was not finding it easy to keep our group together. There was one girl who was forever wanting to stop and look at things, and she was being dragged along by one wrist. I think a porter must have barged right through the middle of us with his trolley. And then somebody walking the other way must have widened the gap between us. Once it did happen, it could so easily happen, if you see what I mean. And the moment I saw that I was on my own, I really did start looking after myself. I moved sideways and fast, got myself on to another platform, crouched down in a space between two stacks of wooden crates. I heard Mrs Elliot shrieking, trying to get the guard to hold back the train. He wouldn't. I heard him blow his whistle, and I've never heard music like that in my life since.'

Mildred was flushed. The memory still excited her.

'I had enough sense not to try to get out through the booking-hall. I went down the ramp at the end of a platform, then crossed a lot of sidings and nearly got run down by a wagon they were shunting. In the end I found myself in amongst a lot of empty cattle-pens: and, to cut half the story out, it was midday next day that some gruff old farmer woke me up, on a pile of sacks behind the brick wall of an auctioneer's office, with the hot sun on me. I've never known for certain whether he was just being genuinely kind to me, or whether he was another of those who saw his chances with me as long as he played his cards right. Maybe by this time I was only looking at any man's intentions from one point of view. And maybe that's a pretty safe mistake for any girl to be making. He took me and bought me something to eat in the place where he was going for his own lunch.

'*The Rook Revived* – that's a funny name for a public, isn't it? But that's what it was called. It had once been called *The Rook*, then it had lost its licence, then someone else had taken it over, and now it was *The Rook Revived*. Somehow I must have got talking about myself – *some* things about myself, anyway – and they gave me a job in the kitchen. *The Rook Revived* – I was talking just now about smells. What would I give, Sergeant Brunt, to smell the smells of *The Rook Revived* again? Soap-suds and mutton stew, rough cider and hanging hams, cheeses and the hot sunshine on a row of beans we had growing up against a wall of the yard. I had to work hard – but I like hard work. George and Nan Dakin. They wouldn't have described themselves as kind people, they'd have thought you were calling them soft: they wouldn't have had me let up on my work, not for a second. But they weren't capable of doing anything that wasn't kind. The time came when I was moved up from the scullery sink to working in the bar and dining-room. I waited on the men in there, farmers and drovers on market day and some of them could be a bit of a handful when they'd got a can or two inside them. Sometimes I had to push one of them off, but it was all in good humour, and as often as not it only needed a joke to keep them in their place. I wish I was back in *The Rook Revived*, Sergeant Brunt, I do straight.'

Someone looked round the door of the cottage and came in after the semblance of a courteous knock: some middle-aged woman of the village whom Brunt had not previously seen. He had to prompt Mildred to get her going again after the woman had gone.

'Where was I? I know: Nan Dakin had a brooch, with a clasp that kept coming undone, and to stop herself from losing it, she'd taken it off and put it down on a shelf at the back of the bar, from where it had disappeared. We didn't think much about it: it could have been knocked on to the floor, even swept up. Then, the same day, something else vanished – a gentleman's snuff-box that he had left on a table while he went round the back. The next day it was a purse from a lady's carriage-bag. We'd had things vanish in *The Rook Revived* before, but not very often, and George Dakin would never have suspected anyone in the house. But the next day, market-day, we were packed out and nearly standing on our heads to get done, when I heard him call my name across the dining-room, and I went back to him in the bar. And there in front of him he'd got all those things: the brooch, the snuff-box and the lady's purse.

'In your hold-all, upstairs,' he said. 'You hadn't even bothered to push it back properly under your bed. I've sent for the constable.'

Mildred's eyes were nearly as wide with distress and hurt as they must have been at that calamitous moment.

'I hadn't touched those things, Sergeant Brunt, I'll swear I hadn't. But I knew that George Dakin was a strict and unbending man. He didn't make threats or play games. I could see myself in the lock-up within the hour. But just at that moment there was a shout from the kitchen.

'"One stuffed breast and two veg—"

'"I'll take it," I said. So I took that plate and swept out with it to the customer. He was a youngish man who'd been in the town a day or two: we had a very good commercial trade at *The Rook Revived*. He always looked specially well cared for – the man you know as Fletcher: Captain Kingsey's man.

'"Well, what's got into Beautiful?"

'He could see I was upset – and I'd let him tease me quite a bit while he'd been coming here. And I'd teased him a bit, too. It was always a satisfaction if a man came back for a second stay.

'"I've got to get away from here," I told him. "Quick!"

'I don't know what came over me, blurting it out to him like that. I was desperate.

'"Trouble of some sort?"

'"They think I've stolen something, but I haven't. They've sent for the bobby."

'"Leave what you're doing," he said. "Don't go back into the bar. Have you got a coat?"

'"It's upstairs. I daren't go and get it. I should be trapped."

"Do without it, then. It isn't cold. And I think the funds will run to a new coat. Go to Number 17, Scarsdale Place. Say that you're a servant from here and that you've been sent by a gentleman to help him carry the pictures. I'll be along within the hour."

'And he was. I don't know how I got across that town. I expected the bobby – who wouldn't have known me, anyway – to come round every corner. Every pair of eyes I met seemed to know all about me, and I expected to hear someone shout Stop *Thief*! at any moment. And I was sure I was going to be turned away from a strange house with a story like that. They didn't know me at Scarsdale Place and I didn't even know as much as Fletcher's name. But they seemed to know what it was all about. The maid who opened the door took me through the house to a white-washed kitchen, and they sat me on a bench and gave me a glass of milk as they might have done to any other Christian girl. Shall I go on? Is this any help to you?'

'It's helping me to piece together what happened in a place called Rowsley. A girl there hadn't pushed her hold-all back under her bed, either.'

'Fletcher came. He wasn't as long as an hour. There were only two pictures, quite small ones, done up in brown paper, and he could easily have carried them himself. As soon as we got out of the house, he whistled a cab: he said we'd better wait to buy my coat somewhere where there wasn't a hue and cry out for me. We went straight to the railway station, where his own bags were waiting for him. I felt very conspicuous on the train, still dressed for waiting at table, and not even a hat on my head. But we didn't go far – the first stop after Cheltenham. And he took me to another small hotel, not a patch on *The Rook Revived*, and I can see now, looking back, how he had everything planned out in advance. In the afternoon he bought me some new clothes. I thought at first that the woman in the shop must think that something strange was going on. But money changed hands and nobody asked any questions.

'Of course, I knew that Fletcher had booked us in at the hotel as if we were a married couple. And I thought to myself, "Well, this is it. This time you haven't much choice, Mildred, my girl. And perhaps something will work out from it." It might even have been worth saving myself for this. You've got to understand. Sergeant, I'd been in a pretty desperate corner, and here I was, out of it. There was one thing I'd fought for all my life: but I was anything but sure that it was worth going to gaol for. Besides, I've got to admit: Fletcher looked a lot younger than he was, and he was being very nice to me. He knew how to be a charmer when he wanted. We'd a quiet little supper together and he bought us a bottle of German wine. By the time he got into bed with me that night, I wanted him to.'

The wheels of a farm-cart rumbled past the cottage: a load of stable-muck for somebody's field.

'I lay there, waiting for him to finish undressing, and I thought of Aileen, somewhere in London. Down in the world now, and you couldn't have said she'd started all that high up, could you? Kathleen and Barbara, two of my other sisters, we didn't even know where they'd got to. My mother, still half hoping, at least she'd be saying that she was, not to have to send Megs and Sally on the night-train. And my father, somewhere, Portishead or Barry Dock, hopeful as ever, plucking up courage, or trying to save the fare, for another trip home. So maybe I hadn't done all that badly for myself. The thought never crossed my mind – it never does occur to a girl, does it? – that Fletcher might get tired of me; still less that this was part and parcel of something the likes of which I'd never heard.

'He tired of me, all right – at about half a minute's notice. One minute he was kissing my cheek and his hands were all over me. And he was clean, he smelled nice, he was strong; I felt as if I was lying in cotton wool, what with the wine I'd had, and a day I could hardly believe in, and I was just letting things happen to me. And he knew what to do; there was no doubt about that. Even that thought was a sort of comfort to me. Then suddenly he stopped: took his hands right off me, half turned his back on me, as if I had offended him. A minute or two later he got out of bed and went and stood by the window. Then he put on his dressing-gown and went out of the bedroom. He was a long time away. When he came back, I'd just gone into a doze. But he said nothing to me. Within minutes he was snoring; and me awake, then, till daylight was beginning to show.'

And what, Brunt was wondering, about Amy Harrington? A very different type of girl from Mildred Jarman. Mildred knew, at least, some of the things she was escaping from; Amy had seen nothing between squalor and the clean white world of her novels. There'd been sin enough – as she'd been accustomed to think of it – all round the edges of her life, but she had never ever begun to think of it as potentially colourful.

'At breakfast time he was sweetness itself to me again, and on and off through the next few days. I say on and off, because he did sometimes seem to forget. He'd go off into a world of his own, as if he didn't remember that I was sitting there with him. We spent the next night at a little hotel in Derby. I can't remember its name, but I expect you'd know it. But this time he booked us into separate rooms – they seemed to know him there. At least, I was looking forward to supper with him again, but he said at the last moment that he had to go out and pay a business call; and he'd already told them in the kitchen just what I could have: *hash*, they called it; we wouldn't have served it up in *The Rook Revived*.

'By now, of course, I knew that he worked for Captain Kingsey, and that I was going to work for him too. Fletcher had charge of a lot of the Captain's business and he did a lot of coming and going between the Captain's two houses, amongst other things looking for suitable servants and bringing them home. There were moments when I felt like making a run for it again, but where would have been the sense in that? No job, no character, the police in Gloucestershire on the look-out for me. Sergeant Brunt – was it from Gloucester that you got your orders?'

'Nothing was taken off the premises in Gloucester,' Brunt said curtly. 'So there was no theft. That's the state of the law as it stands. The Dakins could sack you, but they couldn't bring a charge.'

'I said to Fletcher two or three times during our journey, "Supposing I don't suit the Captain?"

'"You'll suit him," he said. "I don't make that sort of mistake."

'"But I've never worked in that sort of house before."

'"You'll learn."

'And I did. But what do you think I felt, the first time I saw Derbyshire? I'd never lived anywhere, never *been* anywhere before that wasn't civilised. Even in Bristol, there were houses. All this waste space! These rocks! And that train! We had to get out of it before we'd been in it five minutes, while it was pulled up a slope with ropes and chains. The second and third time that it happened, they let us stay in the coach, though they told us it was against the rules.* Then at Hopton we got out and went for a walk along the track because our engine hadn't arrived. And when it did come, that was the first sight I ever had of Thos Beresford. It was as if his eyes lighted on me, and no one else among the passengers. He was staring at me. And those eyebrows: it was impossible to know what he might be thinking. Two or three times, when we stopped at stations, he'd get off his engine and walk the length of the train, pretending he wanted to go and speak to the guard. But always he stopped at the window where I was sitting, and stared in at me.

'At least, I thought in my ignorance, when we got out at the Halt, and the train chugged off round the curve, that was the last I would see of him. He frightened me, and yet, by God, if I'd known what I know now, I wouldn't have been frightened of Thos Beresford.'

---

*Shortly after the events related in this story, a passenger was killed on an incline due to non-observance of the regulations. Very shortly afterwards the L. & N.W.R., who had by now subsumed the C. and H.P., ruled that passengers were no longer to be carried. J.B.H.

Chapter Twelve

'So you made your acquaintance with Piper's Clough,' Brunt said.

'I had to walk up it, carrying the pictures. The men about here certainly know a woman's place.'

'And you had your first view of the Hall—'

'I was taken straight to the servants' quarters. They alone took my breath away – such space! Mrs Palfreyman took charge of me—'

'I've met her.'

'"Let's see what he's brought us this time," she said, and I suppose I must have looked put out, being weighed up like something in the herd that's not quite pedigree, because she softened up there and then, showed me my room, gave me a good supper and sat talking to me while I ate it. I always had to mind my Ps and Qs with Mrs Palfreyman, but I can't say I got on all that badly with her. I had to do things her way, and it was not all that easy at first to guess what her way might be. But by and large I don't hold anything against her. She taught me a lot.'

'About Kingsey and his little ways?'

'I learned most of that the hard way, from Kingsey himself. But she taught me the way I was expected to behave. When she said, at first, "Well, we'd better get you into some sort of shape before the Captain sets eyes on you," I thought she meant just my appearance. But she said other funny things, like, "You'll be expected to do *some* work, you know." The next day I was measured up for my new uniform. All my old things, except the coat Fletcher had bought me, went to help fire the boiler. Picture my surprise when my costume was ready. Black silk, with lace trimmings; they kept an old seamstress on one of the top floors who was doing nothing but keep the whole servants' hall looking like something out of a theatre show. "Am I expected to work in this?" I asked, and Mrs Palfreyman said, "Well, it all depends what you mean by work."

'Of course, I had a lot to learn about manners and table-setting. I may have been a bit surly about it at first, but I'll admit, I needed tuition. The first time I took the Captain a drink in, I set it down on his little wine-table as if I were serving a pint of porter to a wandering sheep-drover in the *Rook*. The Captain turned his head the other way, and didn't look at me again while I was in the room. But he lost no time complaining to Mrs Palfreyman about it, and she spent over an hour the next morning, making me walk a yard and a half to put a glass down on the corner of a table.'

'How well did you get to know the Captain in the long run?'

'That's a long story, and not an easy one. One way or another, I ought not to have been too unhappy at the Hall. The food was good, the work was easy, and there were enough of us to do it. We had plenty of fun together, me and the other girls, when Mrs Palfreyman and the butler weren't breathing on us.'

'One thing, and then I won't interrupt again: were all the other girls there on the same terms as you, or were you something special?'

'I was – something special. That's how they treated me right from the start, though nobody told me in so many words what was special about me. And the Captain took the trouble to tell me once that he was not promiscuous. I don't really know what that word means.'

'Whatever the Captain wanted it to mean.'

'Yes, well, as I've said, I ought to have been able to content myself. While I'd got the Captain's roof over my head, I wasn't standing in front of the justices in Gloucester. But I knew all along, of course, that something else was in the offing. Mrs Palfreyman used to talk about it vaguely. "When the call comes," she'd say, as if there were going to be angels with trumpets. Then one evening, after the Captain had had his dinner, she told Edwards to open some special bottle for him, and I was to take it in to him when various things had been done to it. "And you're to take in two glasses, which means that he'll probably ask you to take one with him. That's if you haven't upset him before you get as far as that."

'I don't know why, but my hands were trembling before I even picked up that tray. There was something about the Captain. He'd never been anything but kind to me. True, if I'd done something clumsy, or said something not particularly clever, he pointedly looked the other way. And when he was disappointed in me like that, he always gave me the feeling that he was, well, only just managing to contain himself. He hadn't lost control of himself yet, but if he ever did, he wouldn't be answerable for what might happen next.'

And Mildred was tough; poor Amy Harrington.

'I knocked on his door. When I went in, he was sitting at his desk, yet half turned away from it, wearing a light dressing-gown instead of his usual smoking-jacket. A bluish green, it was, with a gaudy butterfly worked on the back in silks. And I can't describe what he had on his head. I think it must have been something from his army days, but not what you ever see soldiers wearing now: a little round cap with a red button on top. He made an impatient movement with his hand to show me where to put the wine down. Then he took hold of the bottle and poured himself a glass, looked at me with the bottle still in his hand and didn't seem able to make up his mind whether to pour some for me or not. After a little pause, he did fill the other glass, but he did not offer it to me. Instead, he said to me, "Mildred – it is Mildred, isn't it?" He knew my name perfectly well, of course, but sometimes used to pretend that he'd forgotten it. "Mildred," he said, "I want you to go over and look at that picture. The one in the second alcove from the left. Peter de Wint: *Postmill near Cowbit*." I did as he asked, and I can't say that I thought very much of it: a windmill and a flat countryside. In fact, the picture looked nearly all sky to me. "Now tell me what you can see," he said. "No, don't look round. Don't look round. I want to see the way the light catches your hair while you talk to me." You know what his voice is like, don't you, Sergeant Brunt, always very soft and smooth and careful, but you feel all the time that he's going to break out any moment and start shouting you down?

'"Go on – tell me what you can see."

'But there was no story in the thing – nothing that you could possibly find to talk about. "It looks as if it's going to rain," I said, and he didn't make any reply to that at all. I stood stock still, frightened to disobey him about moving, and then I heard him breathing close behind me – I hadn't heard him come across the room. And then I jerked my head. I just couldn't help it.

'"Stand still!" he shouted, as if he had a troop of soldiers on the barrack square. And then I heard him turn and go back to his desk. I did turn round then, and all the fear and stiffness seemed to have gone out of me. Because he was simply behaving in a silly fashion, and there were limits to what I was prepared to put up with. I thought he was going to continue to be angry, and I was only going to half listen to what he said – but he was hardly looking at me now. He picked up his glass and finished what was in it, and the one that had been meant for me just stood untouched.

'When he did speak again, it was quite quietly. "All right, Mildred," he said. "You can go now." And I did. It seemed a long walk back across that room. And when I got the door shut behind me, and was out in that long corridor again, I felt just as I had done on Gloucester station when I heard that guard's whistle.'

Outside the cottage a man walked by in studded boots. A neighbour's hens were cackling half-heartedly. A plover in the fields was calling stridently.

'The next day, Mrs Palfreyman said to me, "You didn't do very well with the Captain last night, Mildred."

'Well, what was I to do? I'll tell you this, Sergeant Brunt, I think that Captain Kingsey could have done whatever he wanted with me, if only he'd been a little different. I'd have given in to him, I feel sure I would, if only there hadn't been something about him that I can't explain. I mean – he isn't unpleasant to look at. He's a lot older than me, but he isn't disgustingly old. I thought he was the sort of man who would do his best not to hurt me. But there was something about him that I couldn't be sure of – as if he was

89

suddenly going to do something terrible, something you couldn't possibly be expecting. Like when he suddenly shouted behind me, only very much worse – something out of this world.'

She brushed her forehead with the back of her hand. In her rocking-chair the old woman looked completely calm. Could she hear a word that was being said?

'I know it must sound nonsense, but I can't make it any plainer. It might have been easier if I'd let myself go his way from the start. But for one thing, I wasn't going any man's way without some sort of understanding first. And for another, there was no way of knowing what he really did want. Oh! If he'd only wanted *that*.'

Mildred was suddenly contemptuous.

'I knew that sooner or later I was expected to be taken to his bed: but only after he'd gone through a whole lot of things first in his own mind – and I was expected in some way to help him through them – without having the least idea what they were. In some ways I'd almost given in to the notion. I didn't want to. And yet I didn't want not to – not as powerfully as I always had before, if I can make you understand me. But then there was the thought, never far from the top, of what was going to happen after that. Marriage, of course, didn't come into the question – quite apart from the fact that I wouldn't have fancied it, anyway, not with his way of life. And there'd have been other people with something to say about that, not forgetting Mrs Palfreyman. Then there was the thought that he might get me with a child. That was something that wanted a bit of consideration: I didn't just dismiss it out of hand. It can sometimes be made to work quite well, carrying a bastard for the likes of the Captain. But I came down with a big No to that one in the end; too many things I couldn't be sure of.

'Then I knew full well that I was not the first and not going to be the last. And once we were over the hump, perhaps it wasn't going to last long. It hadn't escaped my notice that Fletcher was already on his travels again. And I rather thought he'd be wanting a companion for his homeward journey, if only to carry his pictures for him. So what happened to the Captain's girls when he had finished with them? Somehow, I didn't fancy Fletcher's company, outward bound.'

Brunt had desisted from taking notes while she was talking. But there were some points that he was desperately anxious not to forget. *There'd have been other people with something to say about that, not forgetting Mrs Palfreyman.* And might Fletcher have cast off outward bound with Amy Harrington for company?

'Two nights passed, and the Captain did not call for me. The last encounter had shaken me up, and I didn't settle down straight away back into the ding-dong of kitchen life. I was just beginning to feel my feet again when Mrs Palfreyman came in and nodded knowingly.

'"The Captain wants to see you."

'I looked expectantly at the butler.

'"No wine tonight. It's only company he wants."

'I don't know how I didn't mutiny. Just for a second or two, I thought I was going to. Then Mrs Palfreyman came and put her hand on my sleeve.

'"There's no need to be afraid of him tonight."

'So I went back along that corridor. And the Captain smiled at me as I came in. He was still wearing the bluey-green dressing-gown and the hat with the red button; and he was smoking a long pipe with a porcelain bowl and a green tassel. He took it and hung it in a rack when I came in, saw my eyes straying over towards his pictures, particularly the windmill scene.

'"No – I don't think we'll do a tour of the gallery tonight. I don't want to be told that the weather doesn't look very promising for a picnic. Go and look out of the window."

'I was pretty near to rebelling, but he spoke very persuasively, though not exactly pleading. It was rather as if he were asking for something quite ordinary, like a glass of water or a slice of lemon in his tea.

'"Please do as I ask, Mildred. You really do have it in you to give me very great pleasure."

'So I went to the window and looked out over the trees.

'"Keep as still as you can," he said, "but not so still as to make yourself uncomfortable. I promise I won't shout at you tonight. I just want to look at you. The back of your head really is beautiful. I ought to have stood you there last time, instead of in front of the de Wint."

'I heard him come up behind me, and I felt my head and neck trembling with the effort of keeping them still. But he did not say anything. He came closer and I could smell the tobacco, still on his breath, over my shoulder. Then he put his arms round my waist, hands down on my thighs. I felt my body stiffen.

"You really aren't relaxed at all, are you?" he said.

'I could feel him behind me, pulling me close to himself. His hands were caressing the silk of my dress, moulding the shape of my legs, his thumbs on the inside.

'"Not relaxed at all."

'I wriggled out of his hands – and he held out both arms, wide, letting me go – a gesture to show me that I was as free as I wanted to be. He went to a little cupboard set into one of his book-cases.

'"I hope you don't want to go already? You'll stay for a liqueur? I won't touch you again. I'll wait for you to touch me."

'And I could have done, so very easily. I could have pulled at the knot in the cord of his dressing-gown and watched it fall open in front of him.

'"I think I'd better go now," I said. He nodded as if he understood perfectly.

'"I won't call for you again, Mildred. I'll wait for you to call on me. You know I'm alone here every evening after nine o'clock."

'I felt at first as if I had just got rid of a heavy load. I didn't ever have to come back to this room, if I didn't want to. Did I say *ever*? How long was Captain Kingsey's patience going to hold out? His patience wasn't natural, anyway; he isn't naturally a patient man. How long was he going to put up with me living off the fat of the land in his kitchen, not pulling my weight with his other servants? What was going to happen to me when Fletcher came back with a fresh find? I was drawn to that long corridor, and yet I hardly dared put my foot in it. I could make you a drawing of that study door – from the outside. I can remember every nail in it, every stud. Sometimes I had to struggle not to knock on it. But after all that, what?

'"If I were you, I wouldn't keep him waiting too long."

'That was Mrs Palfreyman, all patience too. She knew stage by stage exactly what was happening.

'In the end, I did go through the door. I knocked, and he looked up hopefully, but finished something he was writing before he spoke.

'"Sir," I said, "I want to go away from here."

'"You do, do you?"

'I expected him to bellow at me, but he stayed calm.

'"Yes. I had hardly expected this, but I must agree that it is probably the best solution. Your stay here has not worked out either to your satisfaction or mine, has it?"

'"No, sir."

'And then he changed his tone completely. He became really acid.

'"And may I ask where you propose to establish yourself as an honoured and non-contributory guest? Of what club next do you propose to make yourself a country member?"

'"There is an inn in the village," I said. "I thought I might go along and see if they could use another pair of hands."

'And for some reason – he is not a man you can say that you even begin to understand – he seemed to accept this. He calmed down again at once.

'"Yes, I think that is a good idea," he said. "A very good idea indeed."

'So I went to *The Crooked Rake*, but it wasn't all quite plain sailing. Mrs Nadin quite wanted me, but Nadin didn't. He called me one of the Captain's cast-offs and didn't want to have anything to do with me at first. He was sure that Kingsey would get at him in some way. That was why he was so terribly worried when you arrived. He didn't want the *Rake* connected with the Hall. But when I said that I would work for them without wages ...'

'You've been working at *The Crooked Rake* ...?'

'For my keep. And to get a character.'

She got up and began to carry the tea-cups over to the old woman's sink. Mrs Hallum signalled to her to leave them for the time being.

'Of course, I know that what really interests you is Amy Harrington. But I don't think I can be of any help to you. I never knew the girl. I never spoke to her. I know that she's no longer at the Hall, but no one saw her leave. I know that Fletcher set out on his travels the day she is supposed to have gone. But he went alone. I saw him go down the valley. I did set eyes on her just once – when Fletcher brought her into the *Rake* while he had a quick drink, the day he first brought her up the Clough. You can guess I was dead keen to see who was going to step into my shoes. And I said to myself: Mrs Palfreyman's going to have to do a fair job of work on this one before she's allowed to carry a tray of wine into the study. I'm not saying that she was bad looking – something might be made of her. But she certainly did not look the type. Fletcher once told me that he never makes mistakes, but he's made one there, I said to myself. She looked so serious – and she'd such a distant look in her eyes. She didn't even sit near Fletcher while she waited for him to finish his beer. She seemed to be trying to make it look as if she didn't belong to him. And I thought to myself, if it didn't work with me, God knows how it's going to work with her. But you can never tell for certain, can you, some of these angelic looking types ...'

Brunt left the cottage shortly after that and on his way to call at the inn, in case Potter was waiting to be picked up there, he ran into one of Thos Beresford's wives, the little fat one with the smile.

'Oh, Sergeant Brunt, we've all seen where you've lodged the young lady, and what a relief it is to the whole village to know that something really is going to be done at last. But why ever didn't you bring her to stay with us? My sister and I would have been overjoyed to have her. We have much more room than Jenny Hallum – and she could *talk* to us. For years now, it's been a disgrace, the things that have been going on at that Hall.'

'It's scandalised you all, I'm sure,' Brunt said. 'But it's taken long enough for an inkling of it to trickle to the outside world.'

'But we've all been so afraid, Sergeant. And this always has been a village to keep itself to itself. But Beresford always has carried on about the things that the Captain gets up to. That last girl – the miner's daughter – he was most concerned about her.'

'Since when?' Brunt asked.

'You'd better ask Beresford.'

'I shall. Of that there's no doubt.'

'But don't make it sound so frightening, Sergeant Brunt. We're all on your side. The whole village is on your side. My sister and I are just about to call all the women together.'

It wanted just something like that. If Brunt needed any impulse to get the case settled, here was a new one.

Chapter Thirteen

First there was Nadin to be tolerated.

'No offence meant,' he said.

'If you're waiting for me to say *None taken*, I just can't be bothered. You're a fool, Nadin.'

'All I've ever tried to do is to keep trouble away from this house.'

'And other people's troubles haven't concerned you.'

'Let bygones be bygones, Sergeant Brunt. You've got this village on your side.'

'Yes, now. And Until.'

'Until? I don't know what you mean – until.'

'Until someone finds he's going to have to be the first to clack on a mate.'

'Kingsey's got no mates in this pub,' Nadin said.

'And what do you know about Kingsey?'

'Only what Mildred told my wife.'

'Leaving me to waste forty-eight hours finding that all out for myself. Come along, Albert, before I spew into this spittoon.'

Brunt did not attempt to outline his morning's discoveries to Potter. It would have taken too long and Potter would have needed too many things said twice.

'We'll go and see what we can find in Brindley's, and then we'll go and talk to the great collector.'

'Of stolen art?'

'Of virgins. Maybe it gratifies the same sort of urge. Unique possession.'

They stumped up to Brindley's Quarter, Brunt walking almost too fast for the older man. But Potter panted alongside without complaint. He had collected gear – Brunt did not ask him where – and had dumped it on a corner of the pile of waste outside the mine: hurricane lamps, paraffin, ropes, a crow-bar, candles and two balls of twine. But before they entered the mine, Brunt insisted on leaping up to the warren above, to see whether anything had happened yet to the abandoned traps. He was too far ahead to hear Potter trying to save him the trouble.

'I was up there first thing this morning, Sergeant: there was still a rabbit, a cat and a hen.'

But when Brunt reached the warren, he found no sign of the carcases: the traps had been freshly reset, their spring-arm newly greased. He immobilised one of them, tugged it out of its anchorage.

'Thos can take a hint. He must have been up here very early.'

'Not early.' Potter repeated his own findings.

'Somebody else, then. I watched Thos down the Clough during my dawn ramble.'

Brunt pulled up the other two traps.

'We'll sequestrate these, Albert. Make long ears in the *Rake* for who misses them.'

Then they were walking down the side of the fissure, lighting their lamps in the lee of the mine entrance, lowering their heads and scraping their shoulders against the walls. Brunt led the way, through the puddle that covered the first few yards. Their boots slipped on the ordure of the bats. The lights from their storm-lanterns showed up Brindley's pick-marks. A nest of baby spiders scurried away over the stones.

But there was no other sign that the place had been visited by any other human agency within living memory: indeed, why should anyone ever think to come in here, except out of passing curiosity, or to shelter from a shower?

After about thirty yards they reached the end of the adit. It simply petered out in the thin end of a funnel – as if Brindley had drilled in a last flagging foot or two in his despairing search for an outcrop. There was no sign that he had been, in Potter's words, *a little naughty*. But Potter was apparently not satisfied. There was nothing perfunctory in the way in which he began to examine the contours of the roof, working back slowly and painstakingly towards the entrance.

'What are we looking for particularly, Albert?'

'I still think that Brindley sunk a *winze* to get into someone else's working.' A *winze* was a vertical shaft dug to connect two levels.

'And you think he went upwards? You said *sunk*.'

'He didn't go upwards. I'm looking for an *eye* and an *egg*.'

This command of the jargon was superior to Brunt's. Five minutes later, Potter found what he was looking for. He called Brunt to look. Two notches, clearly artificial, had been cut into bosses of the stonework, about five feet apart.

'He'd have had a *stemple* wedged across from here to here – a stout wood beam—'

'I do know what a *stemple* is.'

'He'd have used it for a pulley, to haul up his *kibble*. But not necessarily through a hole in the floor. He may have worked down one of the sides.'

He began to examine the rough-hewn walls.

'Here we are!'

Potter had his hands on a boulder that was cradled in a depression between two larger stones. It rocked slightly to the pressure of his weight.

'Yes – and look: it's been moved recently. You can see the difference in the weathering.'

Potter held his lamp close to the stone. There was a difference in the line of discolouration where a half-inch band of rock that had not been exposed for centuries was now visible. Whoever had moved this had not succeeded in settling it back exactly in its original position.

'Go and fetch the crow-bar, Tom.'

Potter giving orders? Neither of them appeared to notice the anomaly. Brunt went back, stooping, and brought the iron bar from where they had left it. He handed it to Potter.

'I shall need a hand, Tom.'

Potter worked with the bar over the top of the boulder, finding leverage for it from behind. After a slip or two he had the implement firmly placed, and though he had called on Brunt for stand-by assistance, the stone came away, once he had found its centre of gravity, as smoothly as the lid of a box. It fell with a thump into the loose toad-stone of the mine floor. Potter leaned over with a lantern into the hole that was revealed. About seven feet deep and twice the width of a man's shoulders, it led down, as far as one could be certain amongst the exaggerated shadows, to a firm base of scree.

'Hold the lamp for me, Tom. Then when I'm down, lower both lanterns on twine, and I'll light your way for you.'

He swung his legs over the top of the shaft and let himself down it in stages, his back against one wall and his feet against the other. When the operation was complete and they were together at the bottom of the hole, Brunt saw that they were at the top of a slope strewn with huge irregular slabs of rock, falling away at an angle of some forty degrees to a natural cavern below. What had happened was a not altogether uncommon experience in the history of the Old Man – Brindley, and perhaps other miners working in from different levels, had tapped their way into a honeycomb of geological origin. Here, clearly, was a continuation deep into the guts of the hill of the same fault which had formed the fissure where Brindley had first struck his pick. Seepage and flood in the cracks where the strata had side-slipped had swilled out this hollow in the soluble limestone. Up in the roof there were cupolas, inverted potholes where the torrents had swirled. But now the system was dry; perhaps because the waters, finding a lower level, had now deserted this branch; or perhaps, when the winter snows were melting, the spot where the two policemen were now taking their bearings was over head-deep in an icy cascade.

There was plenty of room now in which to move about. The recesses in the roof were in some places beyond the reach of the light from their lanterns. They picked their way over boulders into the still larger chamber at the bottom. Sometimes a stone slipped, and once a displacement threatened to start a small avalanche. All movement was dangerous: above them a slab of rock weighing tens of tons was wedged halfway across a crevice, no more secure than one of the Old Man's *stemples*, held between an *egg* and an *eye*. It had hung thus balanced for hundreds of thousands of years.

The terminal chamber was in a state of primeval desolation. And it was terminal. Though the general pattern was of a slope away to one corner, there was no sign of any egress from the cavern – not even a gulley in sight from which the waters might once have made their escape. It was like looking at a vista that no man had seen since Brindley's day: except when one remembered that someone had recently shifted the stone at the head of the *winze*. Nor was there anything to suggest that Brindley's efforts had ever been worth his while – no sign of any seam in the rock-wall, no clandestine entrance into another man's pocket. Unless—

The line of the fault was clearly visible here: in one place you could see the slope of the *way-board*, the narrow seam of clay between the layers. But mostly rock had slipped against rock, leaving unstable surfaces where anything might still happen. Sometimes, an aeon after the cosmic event, a whole wall would explode into fragments at the touch of a miner's pick. *Slickensides*, the Old Man had called the phenomenon.

And there was evidence that this might have happened here. In the furthest corner, where the extremity of the cavern tapered away into the roof, was a tumble of stones that could have happened yesterday – or a million years ago. Perhaps it was through some gap up there, now stopped up with debris for evermore, that Brindley had pursued his nefarious progress.

And the whole of it might come thundering down – in a million years' time – or tomorrow – or within the next ten seconds. Whenever Brunt had been in a mine of one kind or another, he had always been conscious of the urgent desire to be out of it again the moment the task in hand had been completed.

He moved his position from one uneasy stone to another, to take in the chamber from a fresh angle, ready to nod resignedly to Potter that it was time they were back on top.

And then the corner of something caught his eye – an alien object that did not belong amongst this ancient rubble: the corner of an oblong shape: the end of a light traveller's hold-all, in woven cane, still secured by its buckled leather strap.

Brunt opened it with fingers clumsy with excitement, Potter holding their second lamp over his shoulder: a collection of young woman's underwear, indistinguishable, give or take a darn or two, from the garments with which Mildred had belaboured the pair of them yesterday. Brunt fingered briefly through the pathetic pile: the sum of Amy Harrington's possessions, and not an article amongst them of interest or value. He strapped up the hold-all.

'We'll leave this here, Albert, for the time being. I'd rather not be seen carrying it out of the hillside today. We won't share this piece of information with Piper's Fold just yet.'

They searched the chamber high and low for any other relic or remnant of the girl, found not a trace – nor of the passage of any other human.

'She didn't shift that stone off the *winze* herself,' Brunt said. 'And it's time we were back in daylight, Albert.'

They began to clamber back to the bottom of the shaft.

'Tom!'

Potter had put his hand on something that they had missed on the way down, since it was partly hidden by the overhang of a stone. He passed it to Brunt: it looked at first like a twist of dirty rag, but when Brunt unrolled it and spread it over the back of his hand, he saw that it was a triangle of ornate lace, stained with mud and other substances that would probably reward expert analysis: the sort of cap that a superior parlour-maid might be expected to wear when dancing highly specialised attendance on a man like Captain Kingsey.

Potter chimneyed laboriously up the *winze*, raised the lanterns after himself then, hand over wrist, hoisted Brunt over the lip into the entrance adit. They had a difficult task getting the crow-bar under the stone to lever it back over the pit, but managed at last to get it into place though not as neatly lodged as they had found it. An even more sharply delineated discolouration of the rock would now be visible to a sharp-eyed viewer.

Then warm, clean sunshine again: a contrast even more marked and gratifying than Brunt had experienced the first time he had ventured into the mine. A jackdaw, petulant on a crag outside the fissure; a bed of parched nettles; and Kingsey, watching them from a few yards' distance, leaning on his stick, patiently arrogant.

Brunt picked up the traps which they had retrieved and left lying under the arch of the mine. He carried them over and offered them to Kingsey.

'I think perhaps you ought to have these, sir, since we found them set on your property.'

'Where on my property?'

'The warren, above here.'

But Kingsey deprecated the find.

'They belong to a man called Beresford. He thinks he is robbing me. I live and let live. It would spoil it for him if he knew I knew about it. The man likes to think he's an outlaw.'

He declined to accept the traps.

'Would you put them back where you found them, Sergeant, please? As long as Beresford is taking nothing more precious than rabbits, I have no objection. He likes to think he is breaking the law. The least I can do for a neighbour is to leave him his illusions. I'm not a game-taking man myself.'

That depends, of course, on what you understand as game—

But Brunt did not say it.

'And then there's this, sir.'

Brunt unravelled the lace cap, which had fallen back into its twists.

'I wish I was in a position to give you orders, Captain Kingsey.'

'Why? What have you in mind, Sergeant?'

There was no doubt that Kingsey was shaken by the sight of the object. He was even forgetting to be a bully.

'I'd send you round to deliver it,' Brunt said. 'At the door of a terrace house in Tapton. At bath-time.'

Chapter Fourteen

'So perhaps,' Brunt said, 'you'll now allow me to talk to the lad who cleans your knives and boots.'

'I'm sorry,' Kingsey answered. 'That won't be possible. His mother has been taken suddenly ill – somewhere up on the moors near Harrogate. I have sent him home, of course – governess' cart to Macclesfield and fast train via Manchester.'

A moment ago, he had seemed shocked and anxious. His recovery was sudden. The man's resilience was something to be reckoned with.

'It may not be necessary to bring the lad back,' Brunt told him. 'Whatever he knows, you can guarantee he told them all in the kitchen. Fletcher, now – he's a different matter. Fletcher I must talk to.'

'Sorry again. Fletcher's away, too. Business.'

'A remarkable man, Fletcher. He certainly shares your tastes.'

'He's learned, over the years. There was a time when he spent my money on things that I sometimes was glad to throw away. But last year he came up with two minor Jonathan Richardsons of whose existence I wasn't even aware.'

'I wasn't thinking of pictures, Captain Kingsey.'

'Of what were you thinking, Sergeant Brunt?'

'Of girls.'

'What man isn't – ever?' It had the quality of a cynical stage aside.

'We are talking, Captain Kingsey, about a girl who is probably dead.'

And another change came over the Captain – a controlled

seriousness, transparently a pose. It was not the involuntary impression of vacancy that had been his first reaction to the sight of the lace cap.

'I think we had better go into the house to talk, Sergeant.'

'I'd like to go in through the kitchens,' Brunt said on an impulse, wanting to catch an unguarded glimpse of the servants.

'Very well, if that will make you feel more at home, Sergeant.'

Kingsey knew, of course, that Brunt wanted to let his eyes wander. The buxom, human-looking cook was drinking tea between one task and another. Mrs Palfreyman, dignified as ever, but off duty, was sharing this moment at the corner of a table littered with bowls and baking-dishes. The two girls – Emma, who, Brunt thought, might be playing the current lead – and Elizabeth, the one who on his previous visit had described Amy Harrington as *a bit simple* – were giggling at something they were looking at together in an old copy of the *Illustrated London News*. But their activities stopped forthwith the moment Kingsey pushed open the kitchen door. Cook and Mrs Palfreyman leaped to their feet. The girls guiltily stopped laughing. But what did they think they were guilty of? They were entitled to their relaxation, weren't they, when the master was out and the work was in hand? The state of the house was a credit to any corps of servants. So what else was the attitude of this quartet except sheer fear – fear of the very presence of the man?

But he gave no indication now that anyone had anything to be afraid of. He spoke to none of them, but to each in turn he inclined his head, as if in suppressed courtesy.

Kingsey took the policeman to his study. The room looked much smaller now than it had done the previous morning; the staircase and landings less spacious, the expanse of floor about Kingsey's desk, even the desk itself, less vast. There even seemed to be less alcoves and fewer landscape paintings. But all this was an illusion, Brunt knew: any road seems shorter, once its landmarks have become familiar.

He knew that they must look an oddly assorted trio: himself even less of a showpiece than ever, with mud from the mine on his boots and damp patches over the knees of his trousers. Potter was stolid and red-faced from their trudge down the hill, black bearded and displaying no reaction at all. One might be excused for thinking that he did not even know what was going on. Kingsey was wearing a well fitting Norfolk jacket and knee-breeches: uneccentric, unflamboyant – as Brunt had never seen him before. Involuntarily, Brunt's eyes found the painting by Peter de Wint, of which Mildred had spoken.

'Paid for,' Kingsey said. 'I can show you a bill of sale for every item in the house.'

Brunt did not want to be drawn into any discussion of art treasures. They could wait, and it was safer that they should. Somewhere, upstairs, but it would take a dozen men to do justice to the search, there must be exhibits that were locked away for nobody's delight but Kingsey's. And sooner or later, when he saw the jaws of the trap ready to snap down on him, he would have to make a frenzied attempt to dispose of the evidence, most probably to destroy it. Something that the world might have treasured would disintegrate in a stink of burning oily canvas: the whole irrevocable operation triggered off, stage-managed as it were, by a newly promoted sergeant. But it surely wouldn't happen until the very last moment. Brunt felt sure that in the matter of his collection, Kingsey would delay the irreparable until the last ditch. And Brunt wanted that hopeless moment postponed until other things had been regularised. He had hoped to stay away from the subject of art and paintings; but Kingsey had given him no alternative.

'Bills of sale, yes, I'm sure,' Brunt said. 'I wouldn't insult you by asking to see them. Some of them, though, are bound, are they not, to have been made out under the printed heading of one Isaac Mosley, Dealer, of Derby?'

'Naturally. Any collector in this part of the world has to rely heavily on Mosley. You have told me that there appears to be a dishonest side to his business – that is as may be. A substantial proportion of his transactions are transparently honest and orthodox. And those are the only kind that I have ever had with him.'

'Yet he was in possession of your entire Turkish pedlar's collection.'

'You are in a position to make the assertion. I cannot therefore deny it. But I am at a loss to understand how it came about. You and your colleagues are more likely to find a solution to that problem than I am, Sergeant.'

'You assumed that Amy Harrington had made off with the things.'

'What else could I assume? They disappeared the same day as she did.'

'So how did she find her way to Mosley? Had she heard his name from one of the other servants – from Fletcher perhaps?'

Kingsey put on an expression to show that his patience was strained in a most friendly manner.

'You leap easily into a hostile attitude towards Fletcher. He is a man whom I trust implicitly; and by no means simply because I lean on him as heavily as I have to. He was my Colour-Sergeant, promoted on the field in Kaffraria. Each of us owes his life to the other, on this occasion and that. We faced Macomo and Sandilli together.'

'Tight corners,' Brunt said amiably.

'Macomo and Sandilli were not corners, Sergeant. They were native chieftains. But to return to Fletcher. You were saying before we came indoors that he is a man who understands my tastes. He has to. He is my peripatetic major-domo. He has my comfort in the palm of his hand: also my aesthetic well-being, my personal efficiency and my peace of mind. I set exacting standards, as I have the right to, since I also settle the accounts. But I am not an unreasonable tyrant. I acknowledge that any hard-working man in his life-time is likely to make a few mistakes. Fletcher's only bad one to date has been Amy Harrington.'

His tone was bland, but he was not at his ease. He picked up a carved ivory paper-knife, tapped his finger-nails with the edge of the blade, then put the thing irritably away from him.

'You will appreciate, Sergeant, that the tenor of a man's existence in an outpost such as this rests heavily on the equilibrium of his domestic staff. They must be easily contented: a cup of tea must be an event in their lives. They must find ready entertainment in a back number of a London periodical, and they must know to stop laughing when I come into the room. They must be unambitious, otherwise they will quarrel over precedence and preferment. Yet at the same time they must be intelligent. If a girl comes into this study with a slice of cake for me on a plate, I expect her to be articulate enough to comment on my latest acquisition. I do not expect her to dissert upon the latest philosophy from Germany, but she must be wise enough not to deride things merely because they are beyond her comprehension. Also, she must look pleasant. Why should I be depressed by rounded shoulders and filmy eyes? She should wear her clothes as if she were proud of them, and for this reason she shall have clothes of which she has the right to be proud. Those are a few of my essential requirements, Sergeant Brunt. To put it briefly. Amy Harrington fell down on almost every count.'

He raised his eyes to invite Brunt's response.

'And Mildred Jarman, Captain Kingsey – how well did she do?'

'Mildred Jarman was learning fast. I was disappointed when she announced that she felt she had to leave. But when she said that she was only going as far as the inn in the village, I had the feeling that she would shortly be back.'

'Which would have afforded you very keen satisfaction.'

'Of course. I am as keen on my reputation as an employer as is any of your radical paternalists.'

Kingsey dealt with irony by stubbornly refusing to recognise it.

'But sooner or later, Amy Harrington would have had to go, would she not – as have other girls who proved themselves less than ideal?'

'Regrettably.'

'So where have they all gone? Where would you send me to look for them now? In Cremorne Gardens? Or Windmill Street?'

'Sergeant Brunt, I find you disappointingly crude. Fletcher is also in charge of the resettlement of misfits, and his sense of duty is as well defined as my own. Sometimes, of course, a girl does fail to match our standards, though we are usually able to provide her with honest references which will open the door for her into some less demanding household. My own town house, which I hardly ever use, is grossly and expensively over-manned, and this provides a channel for some whom we cannot immediately place elsewhere. And if others are temperamentally attracted to such spheres as those you have mentioned, then all I can say is that they reflect the varied attitudes of society as a whole. Sad; but their own affair.'

Brunt decided that the moment was ripe for specific realism.

'Did you know, sir, that Fletcher shared a bed with Mildred Jarman in a hotel near Cheltenham?'

'Did he, by Jove? I can only say that I applaud his judgment.'

Kingsey laughed, and there seemed nothing counterfeit about it.

'I must say that my own preferences would run to greater maturity. Wouldn't yours, Sergeant? But I've no doubt that Fletcher enjoyed himself. I hope so. I've never tried to hold him on too tight a rein.'

'In fact, the incident seems to have culminated in an act of swingeing will-power on Fletcher's part – to the bewilderment of Mildred. Nothing came of their proximity.'

'You have Mildred's word for it?'

'It seems as if Fletcher's one aim was to confirm her virginity.'

'Having done which he thenceforward left her alone? How extremely magnanimous of him. And wholly characteristic.'

'You must pay him well,' Brunt said.

'He can live comfortably. And he is by nature a thrifty man.'

'May we talk a little more about Amy Harrington?'

Kingsey got up and went to a cabinet of shallow drawers from which he withdrew a portfolio and unfastened its tapes.

'Here, Sergeant Brunt, is Amy Harrington: *Head of a Young Girl*, by Jan Vermeer of Delft. No – not an original. I fear that even Isaac Mosley could not have achieved that for me. But look, Sergeant, at that promising immaturity. That small-boned frame. Those liquid eyes, looking at a man – such innocence as one could not bring oneself to despoil. But for how much longer? Those lips, moist and parted, but not yet ready to be kissed. Until when? Next month? Next week? You never actually met the Harrington girl, I think, Sergeant Brunt? I ask you to believe me, the resemblance to Vermeer's model was incredible. So much so that I got Mrs Palfreyman to hunt out a square of blue and yellow silk to wrap round her head;

a pearl to put in her ear. I set her in the light from that window, and stood back and looked at her . . .'

He was very credibly carried away by the memory. Brunt ruthlessly punctured the mood.

'You're rather fond of putting young ladies under the light from that window, aren't you, Captain?'

'Am I?' If the reference meant anything to him, he convincingly disowned it.

'Mildred Jarman, again,' Brunt said.

'She had a habit of misunderstanding me.'

'And hadn't Amy Harrington?'

'Amy Harrington was an embarrassment to me at every turn, though the fault was not hers, poor child. Poor *Head* of *a Young Girl*. Amy Harrington, I am sorry to say, Sergeant Brunt, was so misguided in her inexperience, as to fall in love with me. There was nothing very much that I could do about it, except to tread as carefully as I could, for her sake. Any little thing that I said in her presence could send her away in agonies of misconception. *That*, Sergeant, was why she took to going out and wallowing in bitter-sweet distress in the romantic surrounds of Brindley's Quarter.'

'You wrote to her father that if she came back you would prosecute her for the theft of the Turkish baubles – though you had taken no other steps whatever to try to retrieve them.'

'Unwise of me – and unpardonably unkind. The truth of it is that when she disappeared, it threw me into a state of mind—'

'The truth of it is . . .'

'Yes, Sergeant Brunt?'

A flash in his eyes, now. It was the first time that Brunt had really succeeded in rattling him. And Brunt knew that he had to rattle him. It was the only way to make him show some of his other facets.

'You'll have a better shot at telling me the truth about myself than I can? Come along, then, man, let's hear your insolent piece of truth.'

'You were warning her that if she turned up anywhere at all and started talking about some of the things that go on in this house, you were ready to put her out of credence and circulation for a very long time. You had your scheme ready laid to discredit her before she spoke. Just as Fletcher – your model pupil – had abducted her from Rowsley with a framework of trumped up charges, and Mildred Jarman from Gloucester …'

'You don't know what you're talking about.'

If Brunt had been a Kaffir, and Kingsey had had a sabre in his hand …

And then he subsided. It was not the first time that Brunt had witnessed his sudden masterly control of his temper. Sometimes in his younger life, of course, he may have left it too late; one of these days he would do so again. But now he actually managed to smile.

'I'm glad that that is what you think, Sergeant Brunt, devious and wrong-headed though your ideas are.'

'Why, if I may ask?'

'Because if that is what was on my mind when I wrote to her father, it shows that I must have thought at the time that she was still alive.'

'Or because that was what you wanted to make people think,' Brunt said.

But Kingsey seemed entirely to miss the flavour of the remark, so impressed was he by what he considered the success of his debating point. He sat back in self-satisfaction and followed it up with a stiff little speech.

'I will throw myself on your personal mercy, Sergeant – though not on your professional discretion, for I have broken no laws according to your book. I have no doubt there are issues you would eagerly like to take up – moral issues, I suppose you would consider them. But I can assure you that I have always been scrupulously careful to stay within your laws. On the other hand, I must confess that my blood runs cold whenever I think of what might possibly have happened to Amy Harrington. It runs colder still when I think that I might mistakenly be held to account for it. And I know how satisfying you would find it to lay murder at my door. That is why

I am going to be honest with you. I make no attempt to conceal the fact that I set out to seduce Mildred Jarman.'

And others.

But now was not the moment for provocative interruptions. Brunt sat prepared to listen. He knew he need not be surprised at this confession. Kingsey was no fool, and Brunt had meant him to grasp that Mildred Jarman had left nothing unsaid.

'And others. I know what you are thinking, Sergeant Brunt, and it does not particularly interest me. Any fool can be a seducer. For me the girl must be a willing party – if necessary must become a willing party, by a process of long-term persuasion. I have neither the physique nor the temperament for rape, and I hope I am too proud for any of the conventional tricks. If, for example, I have in my time offered a young lady a glass of light wine, that has only been to steady her nerves. I did not think that when the Jarman girl left here to go to the inn there was any finality about it. I argued that if she had really wanted to run away from me, she would have left the village. And I felt sure that this was just another stage before her resolve broke down. Once she realised the Nadins' squalor, I thought she would soon come back to me. I was, as you know, mistaken.'

'And Amy Harrington?' Brunt asked. Kingsey dropped his eyes, as if he were coyly reluctant to meet Brunt's, then remembered himself and raised them again.

'One did not think in terms of seducing Amy Harrington. If that is not apparent to you from what I have already told you about her, then I fear that my powers to convince you must remain forever inadequate. And that is not only all I shall say to you on the subject: it is all there is to be said.'

Chapter Fifteen

'The Old Man was up and about again last night,' Blucher said.

'Did you go out looking for him, then?' one of the other drinkers asked. There was a little knot of men who seemed to be permanent features of the bar.

'Me? No, the Old Man can come and go as he likes, as far as I'm concerned.'

'The Old Man never did any harm, anyway, unless it was somebody up to no good in one of his old galleries.'

'That night old Eddie Clayton broke his leg up on the North Scar, and it was not till next morning that we got up there with an old barn door to bring him down, he heard the Old Man walking the Quarter Cord all night: crunch, crunch, crunch. Looking after him, in his own quiet way, Eddie reckoned.'

A pause; and then a more serious enquiry.

'Where was it you heard him, then, Blucher?'

'Up by Benedict's. What's the matter then, Sammy? You getting worried?'

'It's only that I thought I heard something too, but it wasn't the Old Man.'

'You can tell the Old Man's footsteps from anybody else's, can you?'

'Whoever it was set my hens a-flurrying. The Old Man doesn't frighten hens. They take no notice of him.'

The subject petered out of the conversation. They would all have said that they believed in the Old Man, yet anyone who showed in *The Crooked Rake* that he took him too seriously could easily become a butt of the others. No one had mentioned traps missing from the warren above Brindley's Quarter – there was no sign that any two of them together had anything secret on their minds.

'Thos is late tonight,' somebody said.

'Taking time to think up tonight's rappit story.'

'A right old bugger, Thos is. You'd wonder where he gets all his ideas.'

Whereupon Sammy Nall took it upon himself to disabuse Brunt of any misleading notions.

'You need to take some of the things Thos tells you with a pinch of salt,' he said.

'You really think so?'

'He never really did have a rappit that could read and count.'

'You amaze me.'

And that was repeated by someone on the other side of the room: a witticism memorable by the yard-stick of *The Crooked Rake*, a new historic quotation for their annals.

'It's the same thing with half the tales he tells about the railway.'

'Some of them, anyway.'

'Always trying to make us believe that the shed foreman doesn't know he's got an engine out. Half the time it isn't true. But he doesn't like people to think he has to do as he's told.'

'There was one time, though,' Sammy Nall said, 'when the bosses didn't know he had one in steam. That was the time Tommy Ashmore's second was born – or was it his third? They came knocking Thos up, saying they'd have to have the midwife out. Old Annie Smethurst it was, from up on Burbage Edge. Old Thos galloped up to Ladmanlow at midnight, fired and watered the old loco himself and went up the Edge to fetch her in it. The old engine stood the rest of the night in the cutting outside Tommy's, showing a wisp of steam from its blower-pipes.'

'Was that the one she delivered with the fire-tongs?'

Brunt was careful to keep his interventions into their dialogue to a minimum, but there were one or two points on which he wanted to hear opinions, unguarded ones if possible.

'I suppose it's the same with all that talk about his two wives,' he said.

But this was received with a certain glum certainty.

'Oh, I reckon he's stuck with those two.'

'But is he actually married to them? Legally married, I mean?'

'Legally? Thos reckons so.'

'There's always been *talk*,' someone else suggested. 'Some say it's Dora and others say it's Lois.'

'That, of course, narrows it down significantly,' Brunt said.

'Whether it's both of them or neither, Sergeant Brunt, Thos always did have a bit of an eye for the ladies, and when he fancied two of them at once, it ended up with them both landing him.'

Brunt looked sideways at Potter. Potter was thoroughly enjoying the idiotic talk. So had Brunt, the first time he had come in here, but it was wearing very thin now. He turned when he heard someone else coming in, the door sticking as it did for its less practised users. It was Kingsey's butler who come in, carrying an empty flagon in his canvas bag. And this time he did at least acknowledge Brunt – nothing as matey as a nod – but a signal of recognition in his eyes. Respect? Hardly; and not, certainly not, the admission of a mere sergeant of police to social equality. But while Nadin was filling his bottle at the tap of a barrel, Edwards brought out his pocket-book, from which he drew a letter, which he handed to Brunt.

Brunt, assuming it to be from Kingsey, looked at the hand-writing with interest: it struck him as effeminate, which did not entirely surprise him. But when he tore it open, he saw that it was signed H. Palfreyman, and begged him to come and talk to her that evening, on a matter of some urgency.

Brunt glanced again at Potter. He wanted Potter to stay here. He didn't want them to miss a trick if a word was said about those traps. And in addition, Potter could sit through an interview looking so comprehensively insensitive that he might inhibit any real confidence. On the other hand, Mrs Palfreyman's letter might be a subterfuge on Kingsey's part to get him out there alone. It might be foolhardy at this stage to venture alone into Kingsey's stronghold.

'You'll be returning presently to the Hall?' he asked Edwards.

'In about another ten minutes, sir.'

'In that case, we can keep each other company.'
'That will be an unexpected pleasure, sir.'
Brunt turned to Potter.
'You heard that? If I'm not back by ten thirty, come for me.'
Brunt made sure that he spoke loud enough for Edwards to hear.

Brunt had once attended a lantern lecture on *Scenes from the Holy Land* by a committed traveller whose banality of observation was matched only by the monotony of his delivery. *A donkey – a child on a donkey (applause) – a woman leading a donkey whilst pater familias rides (laughter) – a tree similar to the one on which our Lord pronounced a curse on the road to Bethany.*

Edwards could have made a name for himself in that idiom. From the inn to the Hall he kept up a steady prattle without saying a thing worth hearing. Perhaps he was under instructions to engage Brunt in sterile conversation. Perhaps his vocational training insisted on his avoiding the controversial by a blinkered adherence to the obvious. Or perhaps, God help him, this was his natural turn of mind.

'The soil hereabouts is neither rich nor copious enough to support marketable crops.'

And once, on his observation of a zoological specimen which he apparently judged exotic enough to deserve introduction to a town-dweller, he said, in disciplined, undramatic tones, 'A sheep, sir.'

Brunt attempted to vary this diet by inserting an occasional sharp question, less in the hope of enlightenment than as a conversational challenge. The answers were mostly monosyllabic; Edwards combined obstinacy with lethargy – and moved deftly on to more absorbing topics.

'The rabbit, I fear, sir, is a creature of limited intelligence.'
'Tell me, Edwards, did you serve in the Army with Captain Kingsey?'
'I was his Quartermaster-Sergeant. Sir, I have timed the setting of the sun behind that spinney. It takes exactly four minutes for the disc to traverse its own width behind the branches.'

The Hall, when they reached it, was so silent as to appear

uninhabited: a black hulk, that made itself felt rather than seen within the natural envelope of darkness. Edwards knew his way through the grounds as if he were mentally counting their paces along every stretch: several times Brunt bumped lightly against his shoulders as the footpath took sudden turns. The butler took them in by the kitchen entrance, suggesting furtiveness by the self-consciousness of his own movements. If this were the case, then Brunt's visit might have been arranged behind Kingsey's back – and had better not become known to him. And Edwards, then, was at least temporarily in league with Mrs Palfreyman. Brunt's brain was racing in pursuit of innuendoes, a conscious mental excitement familiar to him from several critical points in his career.

The kitchen was deserted, a solitary oil-lamp turned down to the merest bud, and there was a faint hiss of combustion from the cooking range. Edwards did not actually raise his forefinger to his lips, but his whole bearing betokened conspiracy. As soon as the door was closed behind them, he side-stepped towards his own pantry, as if in the greatest relief that an agreed duty was discharged.

Brunt was left standing alone, casting his eyes over the austere tidiness of shelves and table. Nothing was out of place, not a knife, pot or bowl lying about at random. There was a proprietary calendar on one wall, a sentimental picture of children playing in a garden; a month's tradesmen's bills were spiked on a hook; but there was not time for Brunt to satisfy his habitual inquisitiveness. Within a few seconds the housekeeper appeared through the further door, which had been standing ajar. Obviously she had been holding herself ready for his entrance, perhaps had even been standing waiting in the passage.

'Would you like to come this way, Sergeant?'

She led him up the steep treads of a back staircase, taking care to move quietly. But when Brunt, on the first-floor landing, exaggerated the stealth of his own movements, she spoke in quite a loud voice.

'I'd rather we didn't disturb the Captain, but there's little danger of that. I've worked for him for a quarter of a century, and I've never known him leave his study after nine until it's time for bed.'

She showed Brunt into a room that was partly office, partly a store for bed-linen and partly a workroom for minor needlework repairs. But there were also a couple of quite acceptable armchairs and a few framed photographs, presumably of her relatives. It was a room which evidently played a substantial part in her life. She offered Brunt a chair and sat down facing him. He saw, then, that she was barely recognisable from the confident figure who had dominated the line-up in the Captain's study the previous morning. How long ago was that? Less than a day and a half, but within that time something had happened to drain her of colour, to accentuate the lines beside her cheeks: the realisation of something that must have come as an utter shock to her. Confirmation of something she had long suspected? Of something monstrously unexpected?

'Sergeant Brunt, I don't want you to think that I've asked you to come here just so that I can tell tales. Least of all do I want to create suspicion where there might not be grounds for any.'

Her voice was soft, not much more than a whisper, but she spoke fluently. She had not taken one of the easy chairs, but was sitting on a hard-backed one, looking at him over her writing-table, her wrists laid out parallel in front of her.

'On the day that Amy Harrington left here, Sergeant Brunt, I saw her go.'

She paused, as if to examine the effect on him of what she regarded as a startling revelation. She clearly hoped for a response, and Brunt was careful to give her none.

'I saw her leave the Hall. A few minutes before seven, it was. She was carrying her hold-all against her hip and moving quickly and quietly – guiltily, I can only call it. And she went off in the direction of Brindley's Quarter.'

She paused again. Brunt remained impassive.

'You did not try to stop her?' he asked indifferently.

'No. I did not.'

'Although it looked as if she was leaving for good?'

'I make no pretence about that. I was relieved to see her go. She had spelled nothing but trouble here.'

'But you had to tell the Captain?'

'An hour later. When someone else had noticed she was missing.'

She stopped in some unease. 'Sergeant Brunt, you must use your own discretion, of course. I am talking to you as an individual in my own right. I hope you will not consider it necessary to tell Captain Kingsey . . .'

'I can be discreet,' Brunt said.

'He would never forgive me – but I told myself, it was only Mildred Jarman all over again. But that is not what I wanted to talk to you about.'

She waited a moment. Despite the stress, she had not lost her feminine taste for a little dramatic finesse.

'Someone else had also seen her go – someone who did go after her – although, later on, when it was announced that she had disappeared, he expressed nothing but surprise.'

Again a little pause: a semi-colon preceding her climax.

'Fletcher.'

Brunt nodded, unexcited. And did this disappoint her? Did she take a wearier breath than usual before continuing her story? Did it all seem drab and pointless to her now, in face of his unwillingness to be impressed?

'I think Fletcher must have seen her from an upstairs window. I am judging by the short delay before he followed her across the yard. She was already out of sight by the time he had let himself out of the Hall.'

'But he went in the right direction? Like you, he assumed that she was heading for Brindley's?'

She allowed herself a contemptuous little smile.

'Amy Harrington's favourite spot was no secret to any of us here.'

'But well out of her way if she were thinking of walking down the Clough to catch the Fly.'

Though worth making the diversion if she were going to pick up something she had cached there—

'Sergeant Brunt, I had long since given up hope of keeping track with what that girl had in mind. I do know that Fletcher went after her – and was back half an hour later without her. But he did not return through the kitchen. He must have let himself in by the main front door. The next time I saw him, he was coming out of the study.'

Mrs Palfreyman looked at Brunt with peculiar intensity.

'You don't live amongst us, Sergeant, so you cannot be expected to realise all that that means. The Captain's attitude to his study is something that has to be learned by experience, and it has to be respected down to the finest detail. One of the girls – a chosen one – has the job of keeping it clean – but not tidy. Only the Captain is allowed to move any book or object. For sweeping, dusting and fire-laying, the girl must choose her moment. She must pick her time so that he never sees her at work – or coming and going. And no other member of the household is ever allowed in there without invitation. I mean to say—'

In the midst of essential narrative, she found it necessary to stress her own élite position.

'Of course, I would like to think that if ever I deemed it necessary to go in there alone, he would not rebuke me for it. But this is not something that I would lightly want to put to the test.'

'So you saw Fletcher come out? Into the long corridor? Did you speak to him?'

'I said, "What are you doing in there, Mr Fletcher?" If anything had been interfered with, the Captain would be sure to blame the girl, and I would have to be the go-between.'

'And what did Fletcher say?'

'He just walked past me – derisively.'

'Had he anything in his hands?'

'A large brown envelope. And it must have been something he had picked up in the study. He had been empty-handed when he left the Hall.'

Or had it been handed to him at Brindley's Quarter?

'And you did not mention this to the Captain, either?'

'I meant to. Time and again I meant to. But I never seemed to get the opening. One has to be careful, you know, what one says to him about Fletcher.'

'But you've spoken to the Captain about it now?'
She nodded.
'Since my visit yesterday morning?'
'You can imagine that after you had gone, we talked over every slightest thing that any of us could remember.'

Undoubtedly. But Brunt thought that this had all been too glib, too fluent – too pointed and too conveniently shaped. That in itself need not necessarily have a sinister significance, of course: one must expect any woman with this sort of statement to make to run over it more than once in her mind beforehand. But the story had not been told without skill. It had been shorn of any adornment or purpose other than the certainty of incriminating Fletcher. The unknown quantity now was whether she had initiated and composed it herself, in order to exonerate a third party, or whether she was merely acting as the Captain's well-rehearsed agent. Brunt veered to the latter view; it was supported by the butler's somewhat facile connivance at getting him here.

'The Captain told me,' Brunt said, 'that Amy Harrington was in love with him.'

And this thought produced in Mrs Palfreyman a new kind of smile, and not a pleasant one – a curling back of her lips from her teeth that implied a scalpel-like dissection of men's motives.

'Did he also tell you that he was in love with her?'

Brunt looked back at her with carefully controlled blankness.

'But it all depends on what you mean by love,' Mrs Palfreyman added. 'It is an overworked word.'

Spoken with feeling, albeit with cynical overtones. What was this woman's experience? Where had she learned her obviously consummate management of the girls whom she groomed for Kingsey? In what walk of life had Kingsey unearthed her? What was the secret of her complex loyalty to Kingsey? How could she be so patient with his perverse demands? Was she, too, in love with him – another eccentric application of the word? In love with him in full knowledge of and despite his self-indulgences and deviations? Could a woman be in love with a man to whom she was delivering an unflagging supply of hand-picked and fastidiously trained virgins? What other possible hold could Kingsey possibly have on an intelligent and meticulous servant who could clearly earn her keep in many a setting less nerve-racking than this?

'You were saying that the Captain was in love with her,' Brunt prompted.

'Sergeant Brunt, I don't know what sort of picture of this girl you have in your mind.'

Brunt thought of the clumsy, peaky, adenoidal lass he had seen falling over her skirts and boots at old Eleanor Copley's.

'There was something of the chameleon about her, Sergeant. Her very appearance was affected by what was going on behind and about her. The night that Fletcher brought her here – it has always been one of the Captain's strictest rules that he is on no account to see a girl on the night of her arrival. Sometimes it needed the better part of a week. In the case of Amy Harrington, I despaired. I have worked wonders in my time, though I say it myself, but I thought that Amy Harrington was going to be beyond me. Even clothes made to measure would not sit about her shoulders; she sagged away from anything we put on her. Her legs were skinny. The bows of her apron would not stay tied. I kept putting off taking her into the study – for so long the Captain insisted on seeing her, whether I thought she was ready for him or not. I could not think what had got into Fletcher.'

There was energy behind what Mrs Palfreyman was saying now. She had got away from her set-piece, was speaking very much from her heart.

'She was a girl whose very appearance depended on her state of mind at the moment. Hurt her feelings, sap her spirit, and even her health seemed to flag. The colour went from her cheeks and the spring from her step. When she came to us, she was still smouldering with the injustice that Fletcher had done to her at Rowsley. I don't quite know how he handled it – he had been in that district, buying some Jacobean pieces from a family in Over Haddon. I don't know how he managed to put pressure on Amy Harrington, but it had something to do with getting her suspected of theft. I've no idea what his detailed methods were. I certainly was at a loss to know what he thought he had seen in her – until I suddenly saw her looking her best.'

Mrs Palfreyman was more relaxed now, more colour in her own cheeks.

'My heart was in my mouth, wondering how Captain Kingsey was going to respond to that first sight of her. But he was surprisingly placid, saw something in her which I obviously hadn't, put her in the window, then sent me off searching for bits and pieces to turn her into the likeness of a Dutch painting.

'The effect on Amy Harrington was galvanic. It was not merely a superficial change that came over her. To be set apart from the rest of mankind, to be put on a pedestal – any kind of pedestal – that was her fulfilment; from that moment onwards she was in love with the Captain, couldn't take her eyes off him, hadn't even the wits to hide from the rest of them in the kitchen what was going on in her tiny little brain. And, in all fairness, I don't think that anyone had ever treated her with the respect and tenderness which Captain Kingsey invariably showed her. But, of course, it was fatal. In Amy Harrington's case, anything was possible – especially when she first came to us, before she changed – brought up as she was on chapel sermons and silly novels, where the poor beggar-girl discovered in the last chapter that she had blue blood in her veins after all. She entirely mistook the Captain's kindness, took it for granted that he was courting her with marriage ultimately in mind—'

'Whereas what he really had in mind,' Brunt began. But Mrs Palfreyman looked at him with deeply felt accusation.

'I think you ought to be careful how you judge the Captain, Sergeant. You know so little about him.'

'Mildred Jarman did not mistake his motives.'

'Mildred Jarman was a different proposition.'

'You mean it was Amy Harrington who was the different proposition,' Brunt said. 'And how long did it take the Captain to wake up to that fact?'

He could see anger gathering to breaking-point behind the housekeeper's features.

'Do you know how many girls he succeeded in bending to his will, Sergeant?'

'You keep a tally, do you?' Brunt asked her, but she ignored his deliberate crudeness and simply raised a single forefinger in front of her face. 'One, Sergeant Brunt. Just one. And that was long before my time. I don't know the whole story, or anything like the whole story, only what I have been able to piece together from the hints that have been dropped over the years. But it was in his youth; I think it was within the opportunities offered by a country house-party. I think it was with a parlour-maid of the sort that I would be inclined to judge supercilious. I am sure that it is something which he is pathetically anxious to recapture. That is why he sometimes puts on the silly little cap that he wore when he was an officer-cadet. And I am equally sure that he has always failed. Some of them have resisted too obdurately, as did Mildred Jarman. More often they have showed themselves a trifle too ready and he has turned his back on them in disgust.'

'And Amy Harrington?'

Mrs Palfreyman preceded her answer by a well-judged silence.

'He started by taking her on the grand tour of his galleries – and I must say, she played up beautifully. She was not without a feeling for his pictures – in an unschooled way. But it did not go as deep as he convinced himself it did. He brought out lithographs and etchings that he had not looked at himself for years.'

Took her to locked rooms which no one but himself had ever visited?

'He said that her taste and discernment were faultless, all she lacked was the critical vocabulary. He set about teaching her. He said she helped him to see new angles in his own old favourites. He could show the rest of us pictures, he told me – but it was a new experience to him to have them shared. Deluding himself—'

Mrs Palfreyman resented it still. Vivid red spots had appeared over her cheek-bones.

'He found her work to do. He would have her believe that she was really helping him: he taught her how to stretch a canvas and mount a print: inflated trivialities in which she could hardly go wrong after she had spoiled the first expensive few. It was from her naive remarks in the kitchen that I first realised that she thought that one of her precious sentimental romances was coming to life: that he really was building up to ask her to marry him.'

She expected Brunt to share spontaneously her view that such a possibility could not have been considered. If only to keep up the vitality of the dialogue, he declined to oblige her.

'You would not have approved of that?'

She gasped her horror. 'Even at the height of his infatuation with her, he knew that there could be no question of it. Their difference in age, in intellect, in social outlook. She, of course, had read some story of a novelist who had married his amanuensis because his inspiration deserted him when she was not sitting near him with her pencil and her pad. She regaled me with it at length – and him. My fear was not that his wisdom would waver, but that he would let himself be trapped in spite of himself. If she could have inveigled him into making any kind of promise, he would never have retracted. He is that kind of man. And a man can be flattered, which can in some cases be more fatal than physical enticement. Then one evening, she went up to him dressed of her own accord as the Vermeer girl. He was so overwhelmed that he sent her away again, angry with her, angry in that way he has, leaving one wondering what one has actually done. It upset Amy Harrington almost beyond her toleration – and thank God it did. The real reason for it was that the costume accentuated her immaturity. He said all along that she was immature. He was forcing himself to wait, and almost enjoying the self-torture.'

Was Kingsey mad? Were there times when even Mrs Palfreyman's influence on him could not break through? And what was the nature of that influence?

'That was the stage at which I had to take a hand. I have learned in my life, never mind how, a good deal about the way of a woman with a man. I spoke my mind to Captain Kingsey. And to the girl – I took that upon myself. That was the time that she started to mope about the old mine. Mercifully she had started a head-cold, and I was able to change the duty-lists and keep her away from the study. The Captain has always had a horror of avoidable infection. I hoped that the gap would help him to see sense.'

So he had not seen it as easily as she had claimed. But she would have been able, would she not, to threaten him with the collapse of his entire establishment? She would have deserted him, and perhaps taken Edwards and some of the others with her. But many an infatuated man would have settled for the less practical alternative in such an issue. But perhaps she had not been afraid to threaten him with things that really would make him stop and think: she must know, for example, a great deal about some of his art-deals.

'I also had a word with Fletcher and told him to buck up about looking around for some fresh talent. Then I found that in spite of my instructions and the Captain's agreement, Madam Harrington had done a duty swap with one of the other girls, and was waiting on him again without my knowledge – managing to make herself look like a tart in spite of her uniform, sidling up to his chair and giving him the sort of back-street look that he would not have tolerated a month previously. I am afraid I had a scene with him that I would rather not remember: how can a woman manage house for a man who countermands his own orders without even telling her?

'A great change had come over the girl – though not so strange to a woman of my experience. I never have trusted these puritanical types. They are worse than the others when they see their chances open. Nor am I impressed by some of these girls who look and behave like nonentities. They are sometimes the worst of the lot – when the common streak in them is aroused. Amy Harrington was sullen for days, after that first show-down, but then a change came over her. Common is the word I used just now, and common is the way she began to look. She became cheeky in the kitchen; she even cheeked Edwards. Even in front of other people, she was quite shameless in the way she looked at and approached the Captain. She said things to the other girls that came back to my ears: things that did not belong to her, that one could never have imagined on her lips when first she came here. Like, "I am seventeen and he is forty-five, but he'll still have life left in him when he's seventy."

And, apropos of nothing at all, "A wife can't give evidence against her husband."'

Apropos of nothing at all? What of those locked galleries upstairs? Wasn't Mrs Palfreyman forgetting her own loyalties, talking like this in front of a policeman?

'I wondered, of course where she was getting her ideas from. She was saying things that were far too vulgar to have come from her novel-reading. Then it was Tom, the boot-boy, who told us that she had an ally: someone she was meeting, to whom she had no doubt sobbed her misery-story, and who was now encouraging her, teaching her – anything to create mischief—'

So; at last Brunt knew for certain what she had brought him out here to tell him.

'She met him the first time by accident, but before long she was having regular assignations on that slag-heap with that dreadful man called Beresford.'

She leaned back and looked at him, preening herself with satisfaction that she had reached her shattering point. There were questions that Brunt wanted to ask her, but he would have liked time to marshal them. How many times had she handed in her notice? And how eagerly had Kingsey implored her to withdraw it? At what stage had the news been passed to Kingsey that Amy was meeting Beresford at Brindley's, and hadn't he taken any steps to prevent it? Surely Mrs Palfreyman would not have squandered such a chance to denigrate the girl? Above all else Brunt wanted to bombard her with questions which would help him to decide to what extent Kingsey had helped to shape the story she had told him, with its suspect cross-trails and possible false scents.

But before he could frame the first of these, a bell rang on a corner of Mrs Palfreyman's wall. Brunt looked up and saw its coiled metal spring still oscillating.

'Unusual. The Captain. Wants a hot lemon, perhaps. I won't be long.'

While she was gone, Brunt began scanning the room, always in the hope that some commonplace object would have a larger tale to tell than appeared on the surface. But the housekeeper was soon back.

'He knows you're here. I told him you came of your own accord. Please don't let me down. And he wants me to bring you downstairs. Something he wants us both to witness.'

Brunt followed her, and they found Kingsey standing by the kitchen door, which was already open to the night. He was in a sober dressing-gown in dark blue velvet and he nodded to Brunt as if he were neither surprised nor interested to see him on the premises. Outside, they heard the sibilance of iron-rimmed wheels on gravel. A mesh of shadows advanced and retreated as the yellow flicker of gig-lamps passed behind bushes. Then the vehicle came to a standstill in the kitchen yard.

A man handed a girl down from the step of the carriage. At once the coachman moved off towards the stables.

'Fletcher?' Brunt asked. Mrs Palfreyman nodded. Kingsey stood aside with elaborate courtesy to let the girl be ushered through the door. Fletcher raised his eyebrows in over-acted surprise at seeing his master there to welcome him. If Mrs Palfreyman had told the truth, Kingsey usually kept well out of the way on the arrival of a new girl.

She was a big girl, but not in the comfortable country fashion of Mildred. Nor had she any of the sensitivity that Brunt associated with Amy Harrington. She was not timorous, and looked round the kitchen with lively curiosity. Fletcher stepped forward to perform some sort of introduction, but Kingsey cut him short.

'Where are you from, young lady?'

'From Yardley Gobion, sir.'

'Where's that?'

'In Northamptonshire.'

'Take her back home again tomorrow.'

Brunt assumed that this was being enacted in front of him in order to prove to him that the old regime was over. Fletcher gave no indication that it mattered what instructions his master gave him, provided they were feasible and a just reward lay at the end of them. But to the girl, the dismissal came as a different matter.

'Let me stay a week,' she said. 'You'll change your mind.' Brunt had already formed the impression that she was one of those who knew what it was all about.

'You're going back tomorrow.'

'Captain Kingsey, I can't possibly go back where I came from. Those people think I've run away with him.'

'Then he can explain how they came to be mistaken. He is a master of diplomatic persuasion, is Fletcher.'

From which Fletcher did not dissent. He looked less young than when Brunt had first seen him at a distance and in gloomy light. The flesh of middle age was beginning to swell under his collar and strain at his waist-band.

'Fletcher, I want to talk to you.'

No compromise from Brunt now; this was the tone that would be recognised in the coal-mining valleys. Fletcher looked at Kingsey – an appeal for protection; none was forthcoming. But Fletcher was not the man to fold up under the suggestion that he was defeated before anything had started.

'I'll talk to you, Brunt, when I have had something to eat.'

'A man has been known to go three weeks without food,' Brunt said.

And Kingsey did now come to his agent's assistance – but only with a mild appeal to reason and good manners.

'I am sure you will find Fletcher helpful, Sergeant. At least you can treat him as an honest man.'

'Where can we go to talk?'

Kingsey showed them into a little ante-room used for maintenance of his collection: making frames and the paraphernalia of cataloguing.

'An honest man?' Brunt said. 'That's the best tale I've heard since a pit-head check-weighman told me he'd found a butty's wallet in a tub-bottom. You certainly have an honest man's way with young women's hold-alls.'

'I've never stolen a single item.'

'That's perhaps as well. If I could do you for a thimble, I would, Fletcher. But shall I tell you what I'd most like to get you for? I'd like to hang one round your neck for fiddling your own boss. It would appeal to me, that would.'

'You've no chance of it,' Fletcher said. His confidence was aggressive.

'Anyway, the courts are not going to like your particular brand of procuring.'

'All I've ever procured is slavies.'

It would need two girls corroborating each other in the witness-box to splinter that defence. And Fletcher felt safe enough on that score.

'If one or two of them found the Captain was easy meat,' he said, 'that's his affair and theirs.'

'It's Amy Harrington's evidence that I would like to hear. But you know she'll never be going into that kind of box, don't you, Fletcher?'

'Won't she? I don't know anything about it.'

'Well, let's have your account of her last morning here, shall we? That's one of the times when I happen to know you haven't got an alibi.'

'No, I haven't. I was here that day.'

'And you knew she was planning to leave the place.'

'I knew no such thing. I had very little to do with the girl. She was one of my mistakes. The Captain himself will tell you that.'

'A bit too frank and decent for your tastes, was she?'

This was a room in which Amy Harrington had done work for Kingsey. A pair of scissors and a pot of paste were neatly aligned on the table. Perhaps she had used them.

'Listen, Sergeant Brunt, did you ever hear the one about fouling your own nest? What went on between Kingsey and the Harrington girl – or between Kingsey and any of his girls for that matter – was very strictly not my business. I'd have been a fool, wouldn't I, even to look interested?'

'But you'll admit that you'd sleep easier at night with no chance of sentimental confessions from Amy in the offing.'

'I'll admit nothing of the kind.'

'Then give me your account of her last few hours on the premises.'

Fletcher was a quick thinker. He was accustomed to living on his wits.

'I don't know anything. I only surmise.'

'Surmise, then.'

'Amy Harrington ought never to have strayed out of reach of her Sunday School. She brooded about things – hadn't the guts to take them in her stride or the sense to leave them alone. But she thought she could manipulate Kingsey with Sunday School talk.'

'And very nearly did, as far as I can see.'

'She started doing better after Beresford had taken her in hand. You know Beresford?'

'I've met him.'

'A trouble-maker – and a dirty old man into the bargain. A slap-and-tickle merchant, who could talk Amy Harrington's language when he wanted to. You might say that he started giving Amy lessons – lessons in how to get what she wanted.'

'And what do you think Beresford stood to gain from that?'

'Amusement. Titillation. The thought that he might be mixing a bottle for Kingsey. Beresford would ask no more than that.'

'But if Amy thought she was making progress with the Captain, why did she leave the house with her bag packed?'

'I don't know. She was up one minute, down the next. She would put some construction on something someone had said, and it would knock the bottom out of her world.'

'I've no doubt that you can conveniently account for every moment of your time on the morning in question?'

Brunt had decided to sit tight, for the time being, on what he had learned about Fletcher's movements. Fletcher took refuge in an appealing line of near-honesty.

'Unfortunately, I can't. As far as I was concerned, it was a morning like any other. I don't know precisely what the girl's comings and goings were, so I can't even tell lies to fit in with them.'

'Go and get your supper,' Brunt said. 'I'll know where to find you. And when you're wandering about the country tomorrow, taking that lucky girl back where you found her, don't go trying to merge into the green spaces. It would look bad.'

Chapter Sixteen

It was a busy day. This time Brunt really had sent Potter off to Derby, with a crowded agenda – on which one of the most urgent items was to be sure to be back tomorrow. And at least, on the Fly, he would be able to keep an eye on Fletcher and the girl he was taking back to Northampton.

Brunt called at the cottage, to see how things fared with Mildred. She and the old woman seemed to be treating themselves to a late and leisurely breakfast: boiled eggs – and there were a few pieces of china on the table that had a touch of real quality about them. But there was something in the atmosphere on which he could not quite put his finger. The deaf old woman did not want to catch his eye; perhaps there had been some difference of opinion between the two, and she did not want to talk about it in front of him. There was something nervy today, too, in the bearing of the girl from Bristol. She showed no pleasure at seeing Brunt, busied herself stacking breakfast things and contrived to keep her back largely turned to him.

Of course, two such disparate women could not be expected to live contentedly together for long. It was an arrangement that could not be allowed to continue indefinitely.

'Sergeant Brunt, can't you talk them into taking me back at the *Rake*? I'm getting bored stiff here.'

Brunt left the cottage and went on to the Beresfords. Now that the massive sewing operation was over – presumably the effigies were finished – the house presented a changed appearance: warm and clean, though no home that contained so much could ever be tidy. Even more unconsidered trifles from the railway were now visible, including a cast-iron notice-board from the verges of the Cromford and High Peak, notifying trespassers of the maximum penalties – and apparently now used for drawing up the fire.

Dora, the scowling Amazon, was at home, but her sister was not in evidence. Laid out on a sheet of newspaper on the living-room table, the big woman had two stiffened rats, a dead weasel, a mole and a very sorry-looking crow.

'For the gallows – next Tuesday night.'

She was tying pieces of cord round the animals' necks.

'My sister and I are what you might call the stage-managers. This is how the Turks set things up for the landlord and his friends.'

'I know.'

She held up a cord in her fingers, balanced the rat's hind-legs on the edge of the table, then set it suddenly swinging into space.

'Why – Mr William Palmer! Fancy meeting you here on this bright morning. Whoops! Died like a gentleman!'

Now it was the weasel's turn.

'Ah! Mr William Burke. Now just you do as I say, sir, and I promise you I shan't hurt you. Now – toes to the line – and woof!'

She picked up the crow.

'Piper's Fold is going to enjoy this, isn't it?' Brunt asked.

'My sister and I have got all the women together, and we've started already to collect brush-wood and timber. It's going to be the best fire people have ever seen on these hills.'

'I don't think the Turks actually did light a fire under their exhibits, did they?'

'Ah, but you can always improve on the past. We're not bound by anybody's rules but our own.'

'And do you think it's going to do anyone an ounce of good?'

'It's going to do us good.'

'Your husband really does feel strongly about this man Kingsey, doesn't he?'

'And about the Rector. But especially about Kingsey. Sitting there, Sunday after Sunday, with all the back pews packed solid with his whores: a Christian gentleman, the Rector calls him, and can't give us the time of day, just because my sister and I both choose to live with Beresford. Anyway, one of those girls is safe, Sergeant Brunt, I'll give you credit for that. My sister and I, you know, we wanted Beresford to bring the other one to come and live here.'

'Amy Harrington?'

'Beresford used to talk to her when he was out on the hills taking the air. She told him just a few of the things that were going on at the Hall. Yet the saddest thing of all was that the girl was blinded by the Captain. He'd got her in the state where she didn't know her own mind.'

'So who killed her?' Brunt asked sharply.

'Killed her? You do know she's dead, do you?'

'What do you think?'

Dora Beresford began tying the vermin on to the longer cord by which they were to be hung round the pyre.

'What do I think? Well, I'll begin by saying that I hope you're wrong. But I'm afraid you're not. If she'd ever left this village, someone would have seen her.'

'Then who do you think did it?'

She began ticking off names against the tips of her fingers.

'It could have been the Captain because he didn't want her back in the wide world, telling people at large the sort of thing she had been telling Beresford. Then there's that pimp of his. He must know he'll do time if the facts ever come to light. Then there's his brothel-keeper.'

Dora Beresford glowered at Brunt, as if challenging him to deny the allegation. He held his peace.

'Now just you suppose, Sergeant Brunt, that the Harrington girl really had managed to hook her fairy prince. What would the blessed Mrs Palfreyman's position have been then, do you think? Don't you think that Fletcher and Mrs Palfreyman might have worked something out between them?'

'How well do you know either of them?'

'I've seen them both, haven't I? Does a woman need more?'

'A judge and jury might.'

It was amazing, really, that an inhabitant of Piper's Fold should be lined up even momentarily with the law. But then, as far as the village was concerned, the Hall was a different world: perhaps over there they deserved the law.

'Piper's Fold is satisfied,' Dora Beresford said.

'Piper's Fold is too easily satisfied. It's a pity you can't all co-operate and help me to build up a proper case.'

'Cases are your affair – and ours is ours.'

'What a useless attitude. Still, as long as you limit yourselves to lighting fires in open spaces, I suppose all you should hear from me is a sigh of relief. But put me right on one score, Mrs Beresford – which of you two is it that's married to Thos?'

'Both of us, Sergeant. That was the agreement.'

'I know, but—'

'And properly. Done in a church.'

'If you go on talking in public like that, Mrs Beresford, you'll find yourself in unnecessary trouble one of these days.'

'There was nothing unlawful about it.'

He pondered it as he made his way from the cottage. It was a wonder that the garden did not contain a weighing-machine and a penny-in-the-slot affair for selling chocolate.

Chapter Seventeen

'A bit heavy footed again last night, the Old Man, up on Benedict's,' Blucher said.

'They were heavier feet than his again. My old hens were squawking.'

'What time was this, then, Blucher?'

'Well on midnight.'

Benedict's: Brunt had heard them say the name in here before, but it had barely registered. He opened his pocket-book and fished out the slip on which Potter had drawn the seam of ore that ran under the village. Brindley's was marked with one of Potter's stubby little arrows. Anyone could see that the seventeenth-century rock-tearer was not likely to get direct access to the rake from the point at which he had been driving. There were other arrows dotted about, all marking points at which Brindley could have emerged, once he had gained access to the central honeycomb. Potter had labelled some of them: Bentham's Fathom, Piper's Stope, Apple Swallet. But there was no Benedict's. Brunt had to ask – in full knowledge of the danger of showing in the inn which way his curiosity was pointing. But the answer came as casually as the tone he had managed to assume.

'It's a water-gate near the top of the Clough: a drainage level for the whole system.'

'Get your bloody hoof off my foot, God blast your blower-pipes.'

Nought-Four-Nought. Thos Beresford came into *The Crooked Rake* very drunk, cannoning off the front door when it jammed, stopping himself from falling by stopping dead with his weight suddenly taken on one foot. Behind him, Jack Plant was looking unusually concerned, hands like a pair of engine-tender shovels, ready to steady him when he lurched again.

'Where the hell's he been, Jack?'

'We stopped for lunch at the *Lion*, between Hurdlow and Parsley Hay.'

'He's not been driving his bloody train in that state?'

'He doesn't know who's been bloody driving it.'

Nadin drew them each a pint of ale without a thought for the wisdom of adding to their load. Someone made a place for Beresford at one of the tables. There was a general endeavour to make inconsequential talk.

'I reckon thy rappit's getting ready for the celebration, Thos, same as the rest of us?'

'Drunk,' Thos said. 'Drunk as a bastard.'

'Nay, Thos, th'art not drunk. Hast forgotten how much tha supped last Teapot Supper Night?'

'I'm not talking about myself. I'm talking about yon bloody rappit. Pissed as a coot, it was, when I got home tonight. I'd like to know where it's getting the stuff. Of course, he's known for a long time that Lois and Dora like to keep a drop in the house in case anyone's taken queer. I don't know where they bloody hide it, but I reckon yon rappit does. The night before last, I had to get up because I heard someone knocking about in the living room. And buggered if it wasn't the old rappit. It had let itself into the house, and was rooting about in the bottom of the clock.'

Beresford was puffing his cheeks at the end of each sentence, the effort of invention exhausting him. But he found a fresh spate of energy from somewhere.

'I'll tell you a bloody story. I'll tell you all a bloody story. Because *he* . . .'

He swung round and waved a loose hand in the general direction of Brunt, his eye-brows operating furiously.

'*He* was round my house this morning, trying to get Dora to tell him how the three of us come to be living together lawfully in wedlock. Trying to send me up on a bigamy ticket, if he can find nothing else, the bugger is. Well, it won't bloody work, Master

Brunt, because what was done was done legal. And I'll tell you how it came about.'

He caught his tankard with the back of his hand, sent it skidding across the table and beer swilling down over his knee. He did not even move his leg. Someone brought him a fresh pot.

'I'll tell you how it was, and then if there's any bugger here who's mad enough to want two missuses he'll know how he can set about it.'

He belched, held his mouth tightly shut and swallowed.

'I'm courting the pair of them, you see: Lois, Tuesdays, Thursdays and Saturdays, Dora in between times. But it's Dora I'm after, I make no bones about that. But old Lois, you know, she has her bloody moments, too, and she's something to be reckoned with. And damn me if those two bitches don't find out that I'm playing off one against the other. Both of them turned up one bloody night, and I had to sit between them on the top rail of old Josh Pickford's gate. I did my best to make out I'd gone bloody deaf.

'No bloody use. The upshot of it was, if I took one, I had to take the other. Inseparable, they were, and neither of them was going to slave for a man for the rest of her days. Half a man each would be more than enough, they reckoned, the man being me. That was a fair share for any woman to take on. So I've got two women to feed for the rest of my days. And I'm right gone on Dora; but Dora's as set as Lois is that they're not going to be parted.

'So it's all bloody fixed, but on paper, at least, I tell myself, it'll be Dora that I have. Then, if there's ever any question, it'll be all properly sealed and delivered. But I daren't tell them that: I'm not putting any further ideas into their heads. I just quietly let it be Dora's name that the banns are given out in. And there am I, sitting in the front pew, waiting for Dora to turn up in her best hat and beads, knowing that Lois was going to leap out of the porch and grab my other arm as soon as we were fairly up the aisle.

'I heard the organ lash out a bit triumphant, like, and stood up and fixed my eyes on the altar, looking as angelic as I could, with my hair brushed and my eye-brows combed. Then I felt these fingers like a farrier's mate's fasten round my arm, and I thought to myself, Dora doesn't come very far up my shoulder this morning. And I looked round and down, and bugger me if it isn't Lois looking up at me, with that special smile I haven't seen since she saw me bark my shins on Sammy Wardle's stile.

'And their vicar, you know, over at Little Haddon, he's in his bloody dotage. Used to call *me* Jack Plant, half the bloody time. *Do you, Dora,* he says, and *I do,* says Lois. And she signs the register. Her writing's as wild as a black-thorn hedge at the best of times. Bloody great L, with a loop on it that could easily be a D. An O's an O any time of day, isn't it? *I* with a dot over it that's slipped, so it looks like the wriggle of an R. S all rounded out and flattened at the side. Lois Beresford – Dora Beresford – what's the bloody odds? And as soon as we're out in the porch, there's Dora with a bunch of flowers in her hand as big as the Old Man's *kibble,* bearing down on us like a Two-Four-Nought saddle-tank waiting to shunt a coke-wagon off a milk-train.'

Beresford rolled half a pint of ale round his capacious palate.

'If that didn't wed me legally to the pair of them, I don't know any other way of doing it. And if you can find any law broken there, Sergeant Brunt . . .'

Perhaps there was even an element of truth somewhere behind the story.

'Well done,' Brunt said. 'And now we'll have another outstanding yarn, I think Thos.'

'What yarn's that, then?'

Every man's eyes were turned on Brunt now. There was something in his tone that silenced them all.

'You said you'd have an answer for me in twenty-four hours, Thos. It's two days gone already.'

Beresford looked perplexed. 'I promised you an answer?'

'About your traps, Thos. About those traps you haven't been attending to, up on Brindley's Quarter.'

The air of expectation turned into something else now. Some kind of emotional ripple affected every man in the bar. Fear played a part in it, but mostly it was the consciousness that this was a watershed.

Beresford stood up and pressed his thighs against the edge of the table, trying to push the heavy article of furniture away from himself and thrust his way across to Brunt. He could easily have walked round the edge of the thing but physical resistance seemed to increase his determination.

'You keep your hands off those sodding traps, and your snout out of things that don't concern you.'

The table fell over and several men's beer was spilled.

'I shan't warn you again, Brunt. You're here for a purpose, and more strength to your arm. But my bloody traps, and what goes on on Brindley's Quarter, has no more to do with you than my pike-rod has to do with the shed foreman.'

Brunt had no wish to provoke him further, but there was something in his expression that apparently persuaded Beresford otherwise. A shrewd and ugly little man sat looking as peaceably as he could up into the face of a shrewd and angry big one.

Beresford advanced across the room and pulled Brunt's table away from in front of him, raising one hand ready to bring a row of knuckles like a limestone outcrop down over Brunt's mouth.

But Jack Plant was behind him: the fireman with his head as round as a football and three times the size had one hand cupped under Beresford's elbow.

'Better drop a fire-bar, Thos. She'll blow the main valve seating else.'

Plant looked apologetically at Brunt, as if to say that he had spent a life-time calling offside signals out to Thos. A good-natured man.

But wasn't Thos a good-natured man too, at bottom, when you cleared away the clutter that was mostly of his own making?

Chapter Eighteen

The art of doing nothing was as essential to a policeman's skill as the ability to spot the time for sudden action. Brunt knew that he was not going to enjoy the long day before the return of Potter. Because it would be sheer madness to attempt single-handed some of the tasks awaiting his attention in Piper's Fold. By mid-morning he had already broken the most elementary rule of all: he had been alone into Benedict's.

Last night's informant had clearly been wrong in describing the place as a drainage channel for the whole system. It was set far too high in the hill-side for that to be possible. What the conduit must evidently do was to take water off from the upper workings, surplus to the capacity of the lower network, into which Brunt had already crawled with Potter. Or perhaps this had been one miner's outlet before the Old Man had united the whole system by driving his pick into the cavern formed by the natural fault. At any rate, it was feasible that if Amy Harrington, dead or alive, had been spirited down the fissure into Brindley's, she could have been brought out into daylight again through Benedict's – always assuming that the fall of rock which had halted Brunt and Potter had happened after her escort had got her past the spot. A split second after, very likely, sealing off direct communication for eternity. In *The Crooked Rake* they would doubtless say that it was the Old Man's doing. That was how legends came about.

And if someone, mistaken for the Old Man, had been visiting Benedict's on recent nights, could it be because there were traces of Amy Harrington still to be removed? Shreds of black silk torn away against the stone? Perhaps there was nothing there at all;

but someone, now that Brunt had started taking an interest in underground workings, might be under an obsession to make sure of just that.

But Brunt ought to have waited for Potter to go with him into Benedict's.

He knew, as always in this village, that he was being watched as he climbed up the lane that led to the mine, but no one was anxious to be engaged in conversation. Men chopping firewood, women throwing water from bowls out of their back doors, were careful not to see him. Others went into their houses and closed their doors until he had passed. He found his way up to Benedict's and stood for a moment on the ledge outside the slit in the rock, looking out south-eastwards over the hills. From here he overlooked one flank of the Clough. He could see Pedlar's Stump, round the base of which the foundations of a pyre had been laid. Like a colony of ants there was a little swarm, mostly of women, active round the foot of the monument. Beyond that lay the railway and the overlapping folds of the hills beyond the line. A wisp of steam trailed over the furrow of the cutting. Was that Thos at the throttle, the regulator jammed open by his tea-can? Several inclines further down lay nineteenth-century England: trains that ran on time, telegraph stations and newspapers, men at mahogany desks, bearded prison warders and hangman's trestles. Brunt did not consider himself a major prophet, but he knew that the primeval days of Piper's Fold were numbered.

He lit a hurricane lamp and stepped into the jaws of the working. It rose upwards and inwards and had been cut on a much more ambitious scale than Brindley's, the rock-sides blasted out by the primitive method of drilling sockets and leaving them packed and plugged with damped-down quick-lime. Unlike Brindley's, there was room to walk upright, though the walls tapered sharply into the roof, so he had to be careful where he was directing his head. Otherwise his impression was much the same as in the other mine: a dank smell of clay and lime, a chill as he lost contact with the warmth outside. He was helped by the more than usually dry season they had had. But even at that, this was a wet mine, and despite the gradient, the irregular floor held long pools, some of them inches deep. Before long his feet were damp and cold from the seepage through the lace-holes in his boots.

The going was, however, reasonably easy, and he had already covered about three times the distance that they had penetrated into Brindley's when he came to a forking gallery. Rejecting the upper arm, on the grounds that it was less likely to communicate with the main network, he found himself slopping along a level tunnel entirely under shallow water. Except for the tantalisingly weak pool of yellow light cast by his lamp in front of him, the darkness had a quality of surreal intenseness. And suddenly his left foot, splashing its next step forwards, failed to find substance. Gingerly, supporting himself with one hand against the slimy wall, he sought around for fresh foothold. But his boot plunged down below the ankle and the icy water rose to his knee. He thrust himself backwards, twisting his whole body to support himself against roof and sides to face back the way he had come. Another step, and he would have fallen forward into a flooded shaft, and God knows how deep it might have been: perhaps only seven or eight feet, like the winze in Brindley's – or it could be a pot-hole, half natural, half enlarged by man, that sank hundreds of feet down through the rock.

Brunt turned back, convinced now that he was exposing himself, very possibly to no purpose, to a risk akin to insanity. But when he reached the junction with the upper gallery, he succumbed again to temptation: he would take just a little look, go just a little way; as long as he was climbing away from the entrance, he must, he told himself, be rising above the reservoir of deeper water.

It was a stiffish climb. After the first few yards of pounded gravel, he found himself climbing a rough and largely fortuitous staircase of broken boulders. It was not a particularly dangerous ascent, though he tested the stability of each new rock before trusting his weight to it. About twenty feet up he came to a ledge – perhaps an access to the *forefield*, the actual working face of the rake.

And there he found something that looked as if it might possibly have made the risks and efforts of the morning worth while: signs of human activity: a small barrel, a firkin size, known regionally as a *Tommy Thumper*. No relic of the Old Man, this. It was something that had been brought up here within the last few months, its woodwork still solid and its iron hoops still attacked by no more than surface rust.

Brunt came alongside it and examined its contents – not that there was anything left but a sticky inch or two in the bottom of it: tar. And stuck into it was a short, spoke-shaved stick, of the sort that women use for stirring up clothes in their copper boilers, its end tied round with a knob of old rag like a drumstick. He examined the remainder of the ledge, determined now that this must be the limit of his venture. Twenty minutes later he was breathing the air of the village again. Even the stink of stable manure against the wall of a farm-house was welcome to him: there was something robust and honest about it.

He went back to the inn to change his trousers and see if he could borrow a dry pair of boots. And there, to his surprise, it being barely past midday, sat Thos Beresford, drinking rumbustiously, though not yet dangerously under the influence – it looked as if it would not be long before he was.

Brunt did not want another confrontation. He did not ask any questions. It was the landlord, in the privacy of the kitchen, who told him what had happened.

'It seems that yesterday old Thos took a drop too much along with his lunch.'

'It looked rather like it, last night.'

'Consequently he drove round from Hurdlow through Old Harpur with the pressure up and all his taps open.'

'People are saying that the Fly was nearly on time yesterday afternoon.'

'Old Jack Plant, of course, had his hand ready to go for the brake, but he wasn't quick enough to save them going through a crossing-gate that some silly sod of a farmer had left open across the line. The silly thing is that nobody would have known a thing about it. They'd have thought that somebody had backed a cart into it, or a horse had taken a dislike to it or something. There are plenty of farmers along the line who would tell a tale to save Thos Beresford's bacon. But when the shed foreman went round this morning, before old Thos reported for duty, he found a bit of cross-paling still hanging on the front buffer. I blame Jack Plant, you know, for not going round for a look before they knocked off. But the upshot of it is that old Thos has been sacked – he's under suspension, anyway, while it's all being looked into. And, my way of seeing it, there are one or two other little bits of things that are going to be remembered, once those old fogeys in the boardroom start calling for a report.'

Nadin handed Brunt a pair of boots that might more or less fit him.

'Mind you, I wouldn't go saying anything direct to Thos about it, if I were you. Don't go trying to pull his leg about it.'

'I hadn't thought of doing.'

'Thos is vexed,' the landlord said: a mighty compression of meaning into three words.

But Thos's vexation was, it seemed, capable of canalisation. He suddenly pushed his pot away from him and would not have it refilled.

'Later on. I shall sup enough tonight to flood the rake. But just now I've got work to do. What do we want to wait till Tuesday for? Let's have the fire tonight. Let's make it a blaze that will settle Kingsey, the Rector and the Cromford and High Peak for all time.'

It would not settle anything for any time at all: and what of tomorrow? But Thos Beresford was now concentrating the whole of his salvation in the thought of his fire.

'Come on, lads. Why are we leaving it to the women?'

Throughout the morning, whipped on by the merciless eyes of Lois and Dora, the women of the village had been filing up and down the Clough, shouldering towers of brushwood, so that the valley had begun to look like a scene from a production of *Macbeth*. And Thos had no difficulty in whipping up the enthusiasm of the men. Men would have carried huge loads long distances, this morning, rather than risk offence in the eyes of Thos.

Brunt resigned himself to another period of waiting. This time there really was not much that he could do before Potter came back. But patience was hard to force upon himself. He even went to lie on his bed; but idleness was too much for him. He walked down the Clough to meet Potter well before time.

The train was no more than a few minutes overdue. Jack Plant was still plying the shovel, and a driver whom Brunt had not seen before was leaning out of the cab. Potter, large, black whiskered and indefatigable, presented the solid sort of sight that Brunt most wanted to see. The older man started talking as soon as his feet were on the platform.

'A message from the Superintendent: you're to concentrate on Amy Harrington. He's glad there are other aspects of the case that have come to your notice. They will be taken care of in due course, if necessary by other people. You've got to account for the girl, and what happened to her. And I'll tell you what, Sergeant.'

They had to side-step along the narrow path to avoid Blucher, who was struggling downhill under the awkward burden of two broken chairs. The fervour of Beresford's blazing gesture had taken hold of the whole village now, and many combustible articles that were now being thrown out as rubbish would be sorely missed over the months to come.

'I'll tell you what, Sergeant, what with this electric telegraph, there's going to come a time when this country's not going to be safe for a wrong'un to operate in. Did you know that they already know in our office about a suitcase full of rolled-up paintings that was found abandoned on Castlethorpe Station the day before yesterday?'

'Where the hell's Castlethorpe?'

'Somewhere in the South Midlands. It's where you'd join the line if you were paying a call in Yardley Gobion – as Fletcher did.'

'And where he was returning yesterday.'

'There's nothing definite to connect the bag with Fletcher as yet. That will come. He must have dumped it between two milk churns and an advertisement placard. And when they opened it up, they found stuff that's been missing from all over the place for years.

Not in frames, you understand: canvases rolled up in tubes. Franz Hals, is it? Jan Steen? Buggered if I remember all their names.'

'Kingsey getting rid of some of his hotter numbers,' Brunt said, 'and still hoping to get away with it anonymously. At least, I suppose he deserves some credit for not destroying the things. And, anyway, Fletcher and the girl were on the Fly with you. Did you keep track of them?'

'Fletcher over-nighted at Derby: at the *Ram's Head*. He was tailed on the train going south this morning.'

'There's another thing that will have to be taken up with him,' Brunt said.

But now Dora Beresford was coming down the path ahead of them, scarcely noticing the weight, it seemed, of a bursting horsehair sofa. She beamed at them, yawed magnanimously out of her course for Brunt's convenience, and narrowly missed catching Potter's ear with a dangling castor.

'What's that, then, Sergeant?'

'Those Turkish bits and pieces that made their exit the same day Amy Harrington did. For my money they were in a brown paper envelope that Fletcher brought out of the study within half an hour of the girl's going. He doesn't miss a trick, doesn't Fletcher. He knew she'd be blamed.'

'And he sold them to Isaac Mosley? Would Mosley keep his mouth shut just to protect a man like Fletcher?'

'No doubt about that. Fletcher – the boss's trusty – he could be more use to Mosley than the boss himself. And Mosley still has to make a living for himself when he's done his present stretch.'

'So what's our programme now?' Potter asked.

'It's Piper's Fold's night out. We might as well make it ours as well. Get what fun we can out of it – and anything else that may be going. There may be something to be learned from the mob reaction.'

Potter and Brunt were on the scene well before dusk – as the greens of the landscape were just beginning to fade to an indeterminate yellow. A lot of other people were there early, too – including a swarm of children, who were being kept away from meddling distance of the fire by a cordon of raucous women. They did not want any individualist to kindle a light to the pile before the village had all foregathered.

Everything had been made ready: an enormous pile of tinder-dry inflammables had been stacked up, reaching to such a height that only the summit of the Turks' cairn was visible above the top of the heap. The cordon of hanging vermin had been strung in a semi-circle in front of the pyre, and was acting as a demarcation line for the nearest point of permissible approach. Only the effigies still needed to be brought on to the screen. Two decrepit old chairs had been roped to the top of the pile, and were ready like vacant thrones to receive them. A good deal of painstaking effort had gone into arranging and balancing them.

And then a cheer arose from the assembled villagers. The three Beresfords were coming down the ridgy track along a flank of the Clough leading two horses, Thos's and Jack Plant's, into the saddles of which the stuffed figures had been strapped, their faces towards the cruppers. Ungainly and uncouth: caricatures, yet bearing sufficient resemblance to the originals to be distinctly disturbing.

But in front of the Beresfords another figure was running, with shoulders humped and head thrust forward. Brunt did not recognise at first who it was. But then the figure almost fell, saving herself only by thrusting the flat of her hand out against the steep slope. It was Jenny Hallum, the woman on whom he had billeted Mildred Jarman.

Her lungs were near to bursting from exertion and emotion.

'Sir, it's that girl, it's Mildred, sir. Sir, I've done all you asked me to. I couldn't have looked after her better if she'd been my own daughter. But yesterday and today she's not been herself, sir. I thought you'd have noticed it yourself when you came.'

'What's happened, Mrs Hallum?'

'She's gone back to the Hall, sir – and taken all her things with her.'

'When was this?'

'Not half an hour ago, Sergeant Brunt. I got here as fast as I could.'

'And she actually told you where she was going?'

'Back to the Hall, sir. Back to Captain Kingsey. They'll kill her, sir. I know they'll kill her – just like they did the other one.'

Potter was already looking back up the Clough, ready to go.

'I think you may be mistaken, Mrs Hallum – about the other girl, too.'

'Eh?'

She had not heard him. A new ripple of noisy excitement had run through the crowd, who were clearing a space for the Beresfords' triumphant arrival.

A crusty old veteran detective had once told Brunt that his system was to make a list of everyone even obliquely connected with a case and then sit down and try to imagine each in turn playing the principal role at every stage of the crime, from the preparation of it to the deed itself to the cover-up, the evasion and the final curtain. It was an unscientific method, subjective, capricious indeed, but Brunt had occasionally tried indulging in the ritual. It whiled away the idle hours that were a feature of most cases, and sometimes it let in an unexpected shaft of light from the outside.

Suppose, now, that Mildred Jarman were the culprit. Could it make sense? Pre-eminently, the girl did not know her own mind. She had a fierce resolve – one might almost call it an arbitrary one – to resist the blandishments of such as Kingsey; and yet she was sorely tempted. She had been hypnotised by the studded door in the long corridor. So might she not also have become insanely jealous of Amy Harrington?

Might she have killed her for her effrontery of stepping into her shoes at the very moment when she was raging at herself for missing her opportunities? She was physically capable of murder: a strong girl, whilst Amy Harrington had always been spoken of as a poor, fragile thing. But how could she have spirited the body away? Alone, she could never have managed the *winze* in Brindley's adit. But could any person, working singly? Might she have worked hand in glove with Fletcher? Or Mrs Palfreyman?

Beresford drew up the horses in the space that the crowd had cleared. The effigy of the Rector slipped sideways in its saddle. It was a ruthless caricature, a recognisable resemblance, except for round, rudimentary, unrealistic eyes. The representation of Kingsey, on the other hand, was startlingly realistic: a flamboyant dressing-gown, a pill-box cap with a red tassel hanging down by one ear. The Beresford women were handy with their needles; but then they had had longer to work on the Captain; the decision to burn the Rector had been an after-thought, not made until the sexton was given his orders to dig up Thos's potato patch.

'Big moment for Thos, this is, Sergeant Brunt.'

This was the haggard story-teller from the *Rake*: Sammy Nall.

'Yes.'

Brunt did not want to become entangled in ancient mariners' tales at this juncture. Potter was still looking at him with anxious lack of understanding.

'You vexed old Thos, in the *Rake*, last night, you know.'

'I suppose I did.'

'You should never have mentioned those traps of his, up by Brindley's.'

Potter had moved closer to Brunt and was trying to speak to him in a side-mouth whisper.

'Tom, I think one of us ought to go up to Kingsey's place. If you're so keen to see this out, I'll go—'

Beresford was having clumsy-fingered trouble with one of the buckles that was holding the Rector in the saddle.

'A sore point with Thos, those traps were.'

Which was what decided Brunt to give Sammy Nall his full attention.

'Why was that, then, Sammy? Why were they a sore point with him?'

'Well, you see, he'd been warned off the warren.'

'Warned off? By whom? By Kingsey?'

But Kingsey had specifically denied that he wanted to interfere with Beresford's poaching. By Fletcher, then, purporting to speak on Kingsey's behalf?

Sammy Nall spat contemptuously by the side of his feet.

'No – not by Kingsey.'

He was too good a story-teller; you had to wait for the point. Potter made an impatient movement, wanting to be, if necessary, a solitary errant.

'Not Kingsey. By Lois and Dora.'

'Good God!'

'Shall I be on my way, then, Tom?' Potter had not been paying attention to Sammy.

'No. There'll be work for us here any minute now.'

'Lois and Dora, you see, they'd been up to Brindley's Quarter, and seen what was going on there.'

The Rector was safely off the horse now, and a gang of men were chairing him above their heads.

'Thos was giving the girl a bit of learning that she'd never got out of all the books she'd read. What he called giving his playmate a little lesson. Showing her a trick or two when it came to making up to the Captain. Of course, if you saw it at a distance, you might get the wrong impression. We all knew Thos was enjoying himself, in his quiet little way. Silly old bugger ought to have grown out of that sort of thing by his age, I reckon.'

'And those two caught him at it?'

'Crept up on him while he was showing the lass how to move in close to a man's shoulder. They told him what they'd do with him if they ever caught him within half a mile of the Hall again. And they said they'd look after those traps of his up in the warren from then on.'

And had neglected them almost since the day. Even a couple as hard-boiled as that pair had fought shy of going back to Brindley's Quarter, after something that had happened there. They had even offered, through Thos, to make a home for the girl. Perhaps they had told him that they would rather have her where they could see her. And then they had gone up there on the morning of April 23rd to meet her and help her carry her bag . . .

The effigy of Captain Kingsey was now off its horse, and the Beresfords themselves were the central figures in the group that was carrying him. Brunt looked with fascination at the head of the figure, which was lolling un-naturally to one side, as if the neck they had made it was not strong enough for the weight it was carrying. When he had paid his first call on the Beresford women, there had been a row going on – he had heard it through the door – because the head had come off something or other.

'Come on, Albert, those things mustn't burn.'

He tried to break into the group, but Beresford started fighting as soon as he saw an attempt to break up his precious ceremony. The irony of it was that he still probably did not know for sure what had happened to the girl. But did he suspect? Had he suspected ever since Brunt had mentioned those traps to him? He flailed round now, catching Brunt a back-hander that could have knocked him out if it had contacted properly. But it glanced relatively painlessly off Brunt's cheek-bone. Meanwhile, the women were struggling desperately to get the effigy on the fire. There was no hope any more of placing the Captain ceremonially on his throne: the crowd was now milling round between the cortège and the fire itself.

But Dora, taking advantage of her height, succeeded in raising the grotesque doll high above her head and passing it over the crowd to another group who were nearer the fire.

'Albert – that's the one – it mustn't burn—'

But Brunt no longer knew where Potter was. The crowd had hemmed him in now, had jostled him away from the sisters, his arms wedged against his sides. They were all beside themselves with anger, thinking him a spoil-sport. It was impossible to try to tell them anything.

Someone got a flame to the brushwood and the whole construction was suddenly ignited with an inrush of air. The effigy was thrown the final few yards. Brunt could not see over the shoulders that surrounded him.

Then something else seemed to happen to the crowd – a telepathic moment of hush and a sudden diversion of their attention. Someone else's understanding had dawned – someone else now saw in a moment of clarity exactly what was behind it all. Jack Plant had broken out of the crush, plunged through the rope of roasting vermin, half pulled and half flung the effigy clear. It lay now to one side of the fire, small flames dancing along the material in several places – about an ankle and up one arm. And the hessian of the face was crawling with red sparks, like a bird's-eye view of advancing infantry. There was a strong smell of melting tar. Amy Harrington was preserved in it.

The crowd stood back from the heat of the fire. The three principals were now isolated in its glow: Lois with her cruel illusion of a smile; Dora, terror as well as bile now suffusing her craggy features. And between them stood Thos, overwhelmed by a pallid sickness as understanding came to him, too.

Jack Plant beat out the flames that were picking at the figure. Potter stooped with his jack-knife and tore open the torso. Its withered content was not immediately recognisable as a human body. The crowd edged closer. And then by some miracle of mass awareness, the whisper went round. Those in the front tried to push backwards; those behind tried to thrust nearer.

Beresford looked first at Dora, then at Lois, then at Dora again. And then his arms shot out sideways. He brought the two women's heads together in front of his chest with a crash that stunned them both; it was a matter of utter indifference to him whether he had broken their skulls or not. For a moment he stood clutching them by their hair – an act of immense control and strength, for his frame did not sway as he supported their sagging bodies. Then he opened out his fingers and they fell in an uncouth huddle of limbs in front of him.

The rest was not easy. It was not easy getting two prisoners of that kind back into town from Piper's Fold. But amongst their effects, Brunt and Potter were carrying handcuffs and a short length of chain. The volunteer escort was a strong one.

'I ought to have been on to it just that sooner than I was,' Brunt said. 'I ought never to have let them get a light to that fire. It was thinking about Mildred Jarman that put me on a cross-trail.'

'But why did they preserve the corpse?' Potter asked. 'Surely there was somewhere they could have lost it, some-where underground between Brindley's and Benedict's?'

'Albert, I don't claim to understand those women. We don't even have to, do we? Our job's done, the lawyers take over and we, with ordinary good luck, can get back to normal, wholesome villainy. But I think, once they had a corpse on their hands, they were as terrified as the rest of mankind would have been. They caused an avalanche when they were moving the body up out of the cavern, and it must have called on every superstition in their heritage. I think they probably became obsessed by that body. If they had left it in the mine, someone would have found it sooner or later. Remember: Thos would be forever on the look-out. Once the word got round that you and I had been in Brindley's, there were new tales – about the Old Man, up at Benedict's. That would be Thos, exploring on his own account.'

'In that case, he must have found the tar-barrel, and he ought to have guessed.'

'But not enough to be absolutely certain – any more than I was myself. Perhaps he did not really want to be certain. There are some things that a man would rather not know for sure.'

Brunt began to undress, a signal to Potter that it was time he made off to his own bedroom.

'They waited long enough to dispose of the body,' Potter said.

'Because Thos had been talking in a desultory fashion for some time about burning an effigy of Kingsey. The women daren't try to hurry him: he might just have wondered why they were so keen. I tell you, Albert, they were obsessed. Amy Harrington's corpse was with them morning, noon and night. Then the Rector robbed Thos of his garden, and he was really stirred. Remember: the figure of Kingsey was a work of art, but the Rector was a botched job.'

There were few passengers on the morning Fly. The women's wrists were joined on the chain. They did not speak, either to each other or to anyone else. They did not even seem aware of their surroundings. Brunt saw the crags at the mouth of Piper's Clough slip behind a tongue of overlapping hill. There was still a red glow at the foot of Pedlar's Stump.

'So Kingsey and Fletcher might or might not be heading for a stretch,' Potter said.

'They will be. I get a feeling in my veins for the windfall that breaks a case. Those paintings dumped on Castlethorpe Station can't fail, Albert. They mustn't be allowed to fail. Art thefts that have been on the country's books for a decade and more – I only hope they let me do the work on Fletcher in the long silent hours: with Kingsey too far away to be consulted, and any lie I can think of put into Mosley's mouth—'

'Happen Kingsey will see it coming. Happen he'll have made a reasonable settlement on the girl.'

'Happen.'

'Happen they did each other a bit of good last night.'

'Happen.'

Printed in Great Britain
by Amazon